CW00666205

Don't. Even. Ask.
Too. Hot.

NEW WRITING SCOTLAND 42

Edited by
Kirstin Innes
and
Chris Powici

Gaelic editor:
Niall O'Gallagher

In memory of Lorna J. Waite

Association for Scottish Literature

Association for Scottish Literature
Scottish Literature, 7 University Gardens
University of Glasgow, Glasgow G12 8QH
www.asls.org.uk

ASL is a registered charity no. SC006535

First published 2024

© Association for Scottish Literature
and the individual contributors

British Library Cataloguing in Publication Data

A CIP record for this book is available
from the British Library

ISBN 978-1-906841-61-4

The Association for Scottish Literature
acknowledges the support of Creative Scotland
towards the publication of this book

Typeset in Minion Pro by ASL
Printed by Ashford Colour Press, Gosport

CONTENTS

Introduction . . . . *v*
New Writing Scotland 43: submission instructions . . . . *vii*

Shasta Hanif Ali . . . . How to get eggs off your windows
(following a racist incident) 1
Henry Bell . . . . An Obvious Secret. 2
C. D. Boyland. . . . . Saint Sebastian. 3
Colin Bramwell. . . . . . . Devotional Music 5
Eve Brandon . . . . Bog Body, Again. 7
Nathan Breakenridge . . . . Frank 11
Nathaniel Cairney . . . . . . In which two magpies realise they
are not alone 19
E. E. Chandler . . . . Things You Left Me 20
Rachel Clive. . . . . I met your sister today 23
Claire Deans . . . . Getting Rid of Gabriella 25
Lara Delmage. . . . . Crush / I don't cry. 35
Johana Egermayer . . . . . Àite nan Iomadh Loch 37
Graham Fulton. . . . . . . Do You Feel 45
Niamh Gordon. . . . . . . Food. 47
Zoë Green. . . . . Leven Street 52
Lydia Harris. . . . . Robert Dick 54
Benjamin K. Herrington. . . Yo' Momma 56
Michael Hopcroft . . . . . Echoes from Calder Glen. 63
Ellis Jamieson. . . . . Stolon. 74
Ioulia Kolovou . . . . [A Bilingual Dictionary of Loss &
Mourning Weaved with Fragments
from a Journal] 77
Ruby Lawrence. . . . . . . Moulting 86
Hannah Ledlie . . . . Sleeper / The Embroidery 89
Kate McAllan . . . . Gerry 91
Donnchadh MacCàba . . . . Còig Mionaidean 97
Hayli McClain . . . . In All its Moving Parts 98

Jennifer McCormack . . . . . Always, Something is Lost 103

Rowan MacDonald . . . . . 23 Club 106

Crìsdean MacIlleBhàin . . . Litrichean nan Leughadair 109

Carol McKay . . . . Watching Orion While You Sleep /
                       Pawn 121

Gordon Mackie . . . . We Waste Away Like Something
                       Rotten 123

Jane McKie . . . . When we stay by the sea we drink
                       only White Star 125

Iain MacRath . . . . Dheigheadh sinn a dh'iasgach 126

Luke Mackle . . . . Carluke 128

Emily Munro . . . . Frog vs. Prince / To start a fire 133

Donald S. Murray . . . . . Tales of a Cosmic-Crofter 136

Sindhu Rajasekaran . . . . unreal love/r(s) 140

Martin Raymond . . . . . . The Path 143

Aimee Elizabeth Skelton . . . Across the Inner Sound 151

George Smith . . . . Wild Flowers 159

Morag Smith . . . . Renaissance Bat 167

Caitlin Stobie . . . . Deep Dive 168

Tia Thomson . . . . Thus' air mo chuimhne 175

John Tinneny . . . . 923 / A Riddle 177

Jacques Tsiantar . . . . . . Fruits of the Sea 180

Claire Urquhart . . . . . . Dipper / Exchange 191

Lynn Valentine . . . . Midnight, Midsummer, Croft na
                       Creich / St Kilda Crossing 194

Lorna J. Waite . . . . Wee Mercury 196

Catherine Wilson Garry . . . Besom 198

Ania Zolkiewska . . . . . . Shrapnel from Kharkiv 208

Biographies 221

v

INTRODUCTION

There was a sense, building over the months as we read through the over seven hundred anonymised submissions that made up this year's *New Writing Scotland* entries, of the stakes getting higher. Perhaps the way we live now – so publicly, so very much in and around each other's business, so hyper-aware of the world – demands this sort of focus from writers. There is a definite intensity to the writing submitted by this year's cohort. When taken out of context, our chosen title, *Don't. Even. Ask. Too. Hot.*, is not subtle, but then these are not really subtle times.

The outbreak of the Israel/Gaza war happened too close to the *NWS* submission deadline for the writing in this edition to reflect Scottish perspectives on the continuing tragedy of that conflict, but of course this world isn't short of other rocks and hard places for writers to get between. The shadow of climate change and degradation of the natural world hangs over many of these pieces. Nor have the contributors to this issue shirked from showing how the abstractions of politics and economics mean real-life hardship for flesh-and-blood women, men and children. As Shasta Hanif Ali's 'How to get eggs off your windows (following a racist incident)' describes, simply getting through another day with your humanity intact can be a question of practical, determined resistance.

It's also been invigorating to witness how some of the writers in this collection approach these weighty, real-world subjects creatively, teasing and probing at the presumed limits of realism in fiction or narrative non-fiction. Ania Zolkiewska's 'Shrapnel from Kharkiv' presents fragments from the ongoing war in Ukraine, refracted through a choose-your-own-adventure-style looping nightmare; Catherine Wilson Garry's 'Besom' uses scifi tropes of timeloops and multiverses to build slowly dawning horror in a contemporary story of patriarchal control in a heterosexual relationship.

No, the times are not subtle. But the many, varied ways the writers in this book approach them are, and with that subtlety comes space for tenderness, gentleness and the tiny moments of everyday interaction that make us human.

Let's go back to the quote we chose for the cover, and fill in some context around it. It comes from Ioulia Kolovou's beautiful, genre-defying piece '[A Bilingual Dictionary of Loss & Mourning Weaved With Fragments from a Journal]' which attempts to make linguistic and geographical sense out of an immigrant's two experiences of grief in different countries.

'It still surprises me how much we people, we poor people, we poor wee people, whippoorwills, how we fear death and its apparatus and its very name,' observes the narrator. 'Don't. Even. Ask. Too. Hot.'

Here is writing that is not afraid to get up close, to name the things that scare us, but that also reawakens us to the grace of love, the call of place and community, the thrill of music, the consolation of art, and, not least, the presence, despite everything, of the marvellous. Poetry as an act of remembrance – whether uncertain and fearful, or recuperative and sustaining – finds vital expression throughout this issue, including work by Rachel Clive, Zoë Green and Lynn Valentine. Colin Bramwell's 'Devotional Music' takes us on a journey of musical and spiritual revelation.

And, of course, the question of what it means to be Scottish, almost a quarter of the way through this strange and troubling century, is inescapable. Thankfully – wonderfully – it's a question that's been met with a plethora of answers, that blend passion, humour, cussedness, honesty, realism and hope in generous measure. A sense of Scotland overflowing its topographical borders in a spark-flying encounter with the wider world energises Benjamin K. Herrington's exuberant and daring 'Yo' Momma', while the late Lorna J. Waite holds the cosmological and the parochial in a fine embrace. As she puts it in 'Wee Mercury': 'Like tartan, we are all the one stuff'.

Kirstin Innes and Chris Powici

NEW WRITING SCOTLAND 43:
SUBMISSION INSTRUCTIONS

The forty-third volume of *New Writing Scotland* will be published in summer 2025. Submissions are invited from writers resident in Scotland or Scots by birth, upbringing or inclination. All forms of writing are welcome: autobiography and memoirs; creative responses to events and experiences; drama; graphic artwork (monochrome only, of suitable size); poetry; political and cultural commentary and satire; short fiction; travel writing or any other creative prose may be submitted, but not full-length plays or novels, though self-contained extracts are acceptable. The work must be entirely your own and produced without the assistance of generative AI. It must not be previously published or accepted for publication elsewhere, and may be written in any of the languages of Scotland.

Submissions should be uploaded, for free, via Submittable:

nws.submittable.com/submit

Prose pieces should be double-spaced and carry an approximate word-count. Please do not put your name on your submission; instead, please provide your name and contact details, including email and postal addresses, on a covering letter. If you are sending more than one piece, please group everything into one document. **Please send no more than four poems, or one prose work.**

Authors retain all rights to their work(s) and are free to submit and/or publish the same work(s) elsewhere after they appear in *New Writing Scotland*. Successful contributors will be paid at a rate of £50 for the first published page and £25 for each subsequent published page.

Please be aware that we have limited space in each edition, and therefore shorter pieces are more suitable – although longer items of exceptional quality may still be included. Our maximum suggested word-count is 3,500 words, and the submission deadline is midnight on **31 October 2024.**

Shasta Hanif Ali
HOW TO GET EGGS OFF YOUR WINDOWS
(FOLLOWING A RACIST INCIDENT)

The trick is to act quick. The longer the egg sits there,
seeping into crevices, drying into *disgrace*. The harder it is
to remove   *the stain*

- Grab a bowl of lukewarm water with a bit of fairy.
  Not hot water, or you'll have scrambled eggs on your
  windows
- Wash as much of it away with a soft cloth
  (microfibre is best)
- Grab a plastic scraper & one of the toothbrushes
  your mother's kept for cleaning everything but teeth
- Gently scrape the *residue*   off the glass. This
  takes practice. Sometimes you can *quietly* make it
  worse by *spreading* it around, letting it *harden*. It can
  tarnish   the wood, causing *damage, weakening
  the frame*
- Dry sweep the *broken* egg shells. Get into the nooks
  & crannies with your toothbrush. Otherwise you'll
  be picking out *cracked* shell for years
- Repeat when necessary

Henry Bell
AN OBVIOUS SECRET

the universe admits

an obvious secret

in caring, in daily

grinding caring

the universe admits

in boundless care

and worry and sacrifice

the universe reveals

an obvious secret

a line of how many thousand

the universe admits

fractal and recurring

a secret about love

and love and care

that was entirely obvious

and however unknown to me

weeks after that strange new life
arrived in the back room of our flat
your hair stuck with sweat
blood on the sheets
that wonderful nativity
with Kate and the Australian paramedic
who was buzzing because
he had never been at a birth before
and wee Frankie taking her first breaths,
all of us gasping, wet-eyed as we looked
on at your labour
and then that was just the start
everyone tired to their bones, and moved
just from watching awe-struck
but how obvious that birth is just the start
now comes the total sacrifice
her body out of yours and then
you and us consumed by her
bonds of milk greater
bonds of a hundred sleepless nights greater
than any bonds of blood
intimacy and care so huge
that they warp time around themselves
leaving an imprint in every past
so that weeks after as I sit on the subway
and study the face of each stranger
to detect the beauty and terror of their birth
and the care and sacrifice they received
however total and however slight

C. D. Boyland
SAINT SEBASTIAN

Died tonight
it wasn't on the news or in the papers
they tied him to some park railings
in a hospital blue nightgown & shot him full of arrows
left his wounds to blossom
in beautiful possession of everything but life
he'll die again tonight.

This morning
he was Anthony, or Mark or Brian
now they are each Sebastian & all must die
mothers holding back their tears
as they nock the arrow, draw back the bow, let fly
bodies hang apostrophised from bindings
eyes empty of all possibilities
but death

A child brings home a painting
of Saint Sebastian in the playground
crucified against the climbing frame
eyes bright blue, beatific smile red
fletches on the arrows, yellow
the sense, somehow conveyed by painted swirls
of a soul ascending, heaven waiting
his parents burn the painting,
in the garden, late at night
& talk about moving away

One time
the arrows fail to find a fatal mark
a body's carried into hospital

where they withhold medication
'til there's nothing they can do
but leave him lying in an empty room
where he surrenders all his beauty
wounds become open mouths, purple-lipped
that speak. '*Sic transit gloria mundi*', they say
but no-one's listening

Afterwards
they burn the arrows
burn the bed in which the body lay
bury the ashes in an unmarked grave
discuss whether to burn down the hospital
decide not to in the end, but empty it of anyone living
shutter the windows, lock & bar the doors instead.

A cloud of arrows
hangs above a busy street
one may fall, then two or three at once
whomever they strike is now Sebastian
& must die.

Colin Bramwell
DEVOTIONAL MUSIC

1. Gaelic Psalm

How can my voice stand out in such consensus?
Speech and song alike are insufficient
Weathers for the vagaries of grace –
But each thread of this congregation's tuned,
Wound around the preacher's little finger –
He sounds his line, they parrot back their praise.
How can I sing otherwise within this storm
Of vowel and consonant? Luther, Luthier,
My instrument is silence – waves of thought –
Two unclicking sticks to count in God
Whose first chord breaks the string and shoots the bird,
Whose chorus is in harmony with my own:
    A love supreme, a love supreme.
    Lord, show me how to be alone.

2. English Rave

hou come my aye aye jynes the thrang
whun neither speech nor sang'll dae
as tempos fur its ragglish grace?
the club is tuned tae vauntie wunds,
the DJ crossfades banger intae banger,
he does his line and we exhale the ruise.
hou come my aye's aye heard fae inwith
aa this subwoofed glamour? Luther, Luthier,
Luthiest – my body is a tongue, a swallae,
a puir smacked gub aye airtit up,
gurnin in the strobelichts ae His tent,
whas seelence is my treble an my gain,
whas drop retours aa langsamness tae trance.
    Niver huvtae be alone.

3. Scots Ceilidh

When will it be my turn? The bodhrans
trill over lips pulled tight as worry.
Speech and song are both bard's work alike.
I know that I must sing. 'The Blood Is Strong'

by Capercaillie's in the CD rack
behind Al's band – Ruaridh's fiddle-bow
keeps interrupting my view of the jewel case spine.
How can I compare my art with music?

A Lutheran lesson: by Grace alone,
through faith alone. A poem is musical,
word and syntax – my poetry a bothy
with an open door to all who need reminding
that our world and God's still rhyme.
Now let me tell you that I love you, and I think about you
          all the time.

aye – always | jyne – join | thrang – crowd | ragglish – wild
vauntie wunds – elated/proud winds | ruise – praise/flattery
glamour – witchcraft | swallae – big gulp | gub – mouth
airtit – directed | tent – attention | retour – return
langsamness – melancholy

Eve Brandon
BOG BODY, AGAIN

You appear to me as I fall asleep – each night, mouth agape, dragging your torso across the thick carpet pile. In the blue darkness of my room, dissected by the light through the blinds, you almost look alive. It makes me think of that first man to find your body, who saw the crushed hollows of your eyes through the black water and thought that you were newly dead. How he'd cried for you, knelt in that thick, peat mud. I imagine him, red-faced and shivering, as the police told him that you were very old, actually, and so everything was fine.

When you are not manifesting from the damp, shadowed corners of my bedroom, you are laid to rest in a new, shining tomb of glass. Here, now, you are illuminated by tasteful, white light. They've set-dressed your case, complete with a fine dusting of dirt beneath you and a pixelated rendering of a bog behind. The peat has turned you an inhuman grey-brown, and time has done no favours to your dear face, which looks as if it is being slowly, perpetually, stood upon. I can see my own reflection between smudged fingerprints, warped and blueish in the glass. Last night you came to me speaking strange, ancient words.

I knew then that I must come here, to kneel before your tattered body and slide my fingernails through the joining between two glass panels. When security aren't looking, I prise one side free. It yawns open, and your desiccated body looks suddenly smaller, as if it is the remains of a child. I gather you to my chest, frail ribbons of tanned skin slipping through my fingers. In the folds of my raincoat, you are sheltered from the worst of the bright lights. Hood pulled low over my head, I have to peer down into the hollows of my coat to look upon your face. In the muffled quiet of polyester, I can smell the mysterious alchemy of flesh preservation, a sour perfume of malt vinegar and nail-polish remover. I cradle the fragile curve of your skull in my palm and marvel at the twisted shape of your mouth against my neck.

No-one stops me on the way out, thinking you a swaddled baby or a swollen belly. I sit on the marble steps and gaze out on the tidal push and pull of city traffic. I try to plan the days ahead. I can conjure up a map of the surviving peatlands of this island, let it blaze before me across the grey haze of this city in spring. I will take us south, I decide, to where we both grew up. The marshes have been drained, the dark earth eaten up, but there is a way, I know, to bring us both home.

We sit for many hours on the Megabus, your hand (?) in mine. The heating is broken and the air shivers with warmth. Our fellow passengers take on a fevered, glaze-eyed look to them, as cold, brown, British countryside whips past the window. I can feel something seep into the damp fabric of my t-shirt and I begin to worry about you, and think about what it must be like to rot so many years after your death. The other passengers wince from me, as if I am about to bite, or talk about the gospel. I want to beckon them closer, allow them to marvel, quietly, at the withered smallness of your body. I want to tell them that it was, as it is now, late spring when you died. That there is, as in ours, mistletoe pollen and assorted grains within the collapsed space of your stomach. But without your glass box, they would not understand the miracle of you.

Together we brave the worst atrocities of the M6, clutched close to one another. That night, in the strange, uncanny light of our room, I fall into bed with you. In this quiet intimacy, it feels profane to look upon your face. I pull the sheets around us, which are bleached so white and stiff as to feel uncleanly against the skin. I extricate a pillow from its case so that I can try to shroud your head in the same cloth, but it looks too much like you are on the gallows, or the ghost at a Halloween party.

I think about what it would have meant to meet you in the shitty local club of our hometown. Instead of a Travelodge, we find each other in the bathroom, making fleeting eye contact in the mirror as we wash our hands. Around the scratches and gouges in its surface and the haze of alcohol, we will recognise each other as a friend of a friend of a friend. And over the thud of ABBA in the next room, I'll be able to speak and make you smile.

But we have missed each other, you and I, by a singular hairsbreadth of geologic time.

I turn you around so that you are facing the window, and so I can pretend that the collected heat of us is something tender, wholesome, permanent. My eyes slide half-closed, and I fall asleep watching the assorted lights of the motorway leap across the creeping wetness of your skin.

I hunt the countryside for signs of a place for us. Articulated lorries whip past us – great, snub-nosed beasts of burden – and their headlights flash and smear in the growing light. I can hear police sirens in the distance and worry, just for a moment, that I will be shot like a deer on the motorway. I blink, I hold you tighter and I push onward through the lanes of traffic. Someone leans hard on their horn as my coat is pulled flush with a smooth and shining flank. I throw us over a fence, barbed wire latching deep like a fishhook into one of your many, disintegrating ribbons.

This land is quieter than the one you knew. It is, of course, a veritable haunted house of waterfowl. It must be terrifying, that absence. I think I'd like to hear you describe the leaves of plants that no longer grow here, but I wouldn't want to upset you. I look instead to the sheep embedded in the neighbouring hillside, and I consider a subspecies of never-before, never-again wolves, who hunt the marshes on webbed paws. An impossible world, in which me and you might never have existed. Yet it seeps through the reeds and up around the soles of my trainers.

I'm not sad though. These things happen. And you would have loved plastic, pineapple, and Schnapps.

Mouth open in a wheeze, hands otherwise occupied by your body, my journey is not graceful. With each fall I feel more panicked and I struggle and flail and trip once more. I take on a locomotive pace, with each fall propelling me further into the marshes. I am fenced in on all sides by walls of cut peat, stacked like sugar cubes into neat little pyramids. The taste of mud on my tongue reminds me of beetroot and petrol. I juggle the remains of your body, freeing one hand to grasp the reeds that frame our path and pull myself ever onwards.

I find a spot amongst yellow grasses where the waters are syrupy, dark and deep. I kneel and regain my breath in great, heaving gulps. I wish bitterly that the weather was more atmospheric, or that I could say some words that we'd both understand. I kiss your cheek, like you are some distant, obligatory relation. When I lower you into the water, your body does not make a sound.

I hope that this soothes the frantic heat of your rotting flesh. That the chemicals that they have anointed you with do not poison these waters. That you are held close by the mud and by the dark. That you are never seen again.

I hope, most of all, that it is okay if I lie here, next to you, for some short while.

Nathan Breakenridge
FRANK

Deb woke to an empty bed with daylight forcing itself through the crack in the curtains. She swung her legs out from under the duvet and stepped into her slippers, pulled a robe from the handle of the wardrobe. Bloody man, she said.

When she drew the curtains the early sun felt warm on her face and she stood in it blinking until she could see his pillows lodged between the mattress and the bedside table. She set them right and threw the duvet back into place and went out onto the landing.

All the doors were still closed. The light from the window behind her threw shadows of her legs onto the carpet and the opposite wall. Somewhere downstairs the kettle was boiling. She followed the sound to the bottom of the stairs and stopped and called his name.

Judy was sitting at the kitchen table propping up two slices of toast on her plate like a tent.

Have you seen your father?

Is he no still asleep?

If he'd been in the bed with me I'd know where he was, wouldn't I?

Judy shrugged and looked back at her phone. The case was shaped like a poke of chips, too big for her hand. Have you checked both toilets?

Deb went back into the hall and chapped the door under the stairs. Frank? You in the lavvy? She went upstairs and did the same. She tried the door but it was open and the bathroom empty. She went back downstairs.

Are you sure you never heard him go out?

Judy was stirring coffee with one hand, checking the temperature of her toast with the other. No since I got up.

Why are you up? Are you no off the day?

I couldnae sleep so I got up. Is he in the garage?

She checked but he wasn't. His car was in the driveway. His boots were by the door.

*

After poaching an egg and eating it with toast Deb made tea to take upstairs. She sipped it while she put in rollers and got dressed. Then she moved across the upper landing opening doors and blinds and curtains. In Judy's room she had to wade through piles of clothes to pull her duvet flat. She upset a stack of empty pill packets on the bedside table and so gathered them up and held them against her belly. There was an empty Irn-Bru bottle on the floor and she tried to toss it with her free hand into the bin by the door. It bounced off the pile of tissues and makeup wipes and rolled off down the landing. She emptied the packets into the bin and carried the bottle and the bin back downstairs.

Judy was still sitting in front of her empty plate, staring into her phone. You'll need to order more of your Femoston, Deb said. She tipped the bedroom bin into the kitchen bin and took out the bag and tied the top of it. She stood holding it for a moment. Where the hell is he? she said.

Is he working?

Deb opened the back door and leaned around the frame with her empty hand to lift the lid of the outside bin and swung the bag in and shut the door again. He never told me if he was, she said.

Have you phoned him?

Deb stood and looked at her daughter for a moment and then went to pick up her phone charging on the worktop.

You shouldnae leave that charging overnight, said Judy.

Deb shooed her with one hand and brought the phone to her ear. After a few seconds the tinny old-fashioned bell of his ringtone made them both jump. Deb followed the sound upstairs and into the bedroom. She found the phone rattling on his bedside table and carried it back downstairs.

Bugger must have left it, she said. She set the phone down on the table in front of Judy. Judy looked up and then back down at her own phone.

Is this all you're gonnae do with your day off? her mother asked.

I might have a bath.

Have you no college work?

Judy shrugged. Deb blew out through her nose and started to ferry plates to the dishwasher. You don't seem to be taking it very seriously Jack. Your da'd this house when he was your age.

Judy. My name's Judy.

Judy? She blinked and shook her head. Oh I'm sorry Judy. Judy I'm sorry. She turned to look at her. I'm thinking about your da, I'm distracted. I'm sorry.

Judy stood up from the table and went upstairs. She finished stacking the dishwasher and shut it and stood with her back to the counter and closed her eyes.

*

Deb walked into the living room with her phone in her hand. The office says they've never given him anything. He'd said that to me as well. Kevin's no spoke to him either. I phoned the Strathie but it's shut till four anyhow. How long is it before you can report someone missing?

Twenty-four hours I think.

Gonnae check?

Judy's acrylic nails clicked against the phone screen. She was wearing a thick pink dressing gown and had her hair up in a towel. Aye twenty-four hours, she said.

Deb looked at the clock. That's nearly one o'clock, how long's that?

Depends when you saw him last.

Last night before I went to my bed.

Did you hear him come to bed?

She shook her head. I conked out, I was done in. Emma'd been round with the weans.

It won't be twenty-four hours till the night then.

Did you no see him?

I was in late.

And yet up at the crack of dawn. Wonders never cease.

She sat down beside her daughter on the couch. It's no like him Judy. What if he's hurt hisself?

Judy leaned over and picked up his phone from the coffee table and tapped the screen. Did you see that? She handed it to her mother.

There was an unread text on the screen from a number she didn't recognise. An address.

It buzzed a wee minute ago, Judy said.

Is that in town?

Judy took the phone back and looked at it. Aye, she said, Near the centre.

Right.

*

Is he buying gear do you think? Or having an affair?

This is a man who wore leather trousers to get a vasectomy. He's no that clever.

I mean he left his phone so – wait, did he actually?

This is the first time in twenty year I've no known exactly where he was.

They were standing across the road from a block of tenement flats near the city centre. They'd been watching the door through the afternoon traffic for a while. No one had come or gone. They crossed the road and stood in front of the door, lacquered and blood-red.

Flat ten aye?

Judy's head dropped back. Does that mean it's up the top?

Her mother leaned in to look at the panel of buttons on the wall. The button for number ten was missing.

Buzz one of the others and ask? Judy said.

Deb frowned and turned back to the door and pushed it. It swung open. They went inside.

The close was dark and full of a sour mineral smell. Metal and damp wood and urine. They followed a short corridor towards the stairs, past a room full of bins and balls of tinfoil. The first two flats were at either side of the foot of the stairs. One door was ajar, a laundry basket full of children's toys just visible through the gap.

It stinks, Judy said.

Deb nodded and started up the stairs. Your granny used to live in one of these, she said. Before you were born.

The walls were moss green and peeling. They could hear soft voices from one of the floors above. Someone singing badly. Judy stopped to pant on the first landing. Right there's two flats on every floor, how many's that to go?

You should be fitter than me, Deb said, and started up the next flight. These are needing a good sweep. She kicked some dead leaves from the bottom step onto the landing.

The only light came from the milky windows between each floor. Deb couldn't decide where the singing was coming from, whether it was a man or a woman. They were slow going up, peching and red and squinting in the gloom.

On the third floor they stopped. Above them on the halfway landing there was a man slumped against the wall. He was only wearing one shoe and the window behind him lit his face so the features seemed blurred. Deb realised after a moment that he was bleeding, his head open and running down over his eyes and around his nose. He was breathing quickly and his eyes were open, staring past them at the landing below.

It's okay we've phoned the polis.

A woman was leaning over the banister of the next floor up. Yous can come up. He won't move. Try no to look at him.

Judy looked at her mother and started to move up the stairs. They had to step over his legs when they passed him. Despite herself Deb stared at him as they passed. He had dropped his chin to his chest and between the shadows and the blood she couldn't make out any of his features. Looking down, she saw that he had pissed himself. There was blood from his head spattered down the steps above him.

Two women were standing at the open door of one of the flats. Junkie, one of them said. He's shot up and tried to go down the stair. We've phoned the polis.

The main door doesnae lock so we get a lot of them, the other said.

Has that happened before?

No like that. But we've had to phone the polis before.

I hope he's all right, Judy said.

They stood there for a moment while the women watched them. The one on the right stared hard at Judy and wouldn't look away.

We're looking for number ten, Deb said.

I don't think there is one. We're in seven.

There's no one on the buzzer.

There's only one more upstairs.

Well. It must be that one we're after.

The women stood and watched them as they passed. Deb could hear them whispering behind them.

The next stairway was narrower than the others. It ran along the wall up to a single door and when they reached it Judy stopped. Are they no right?

What?

We've done four floors but there's only one up here.

Deb frowned.

So this is number nine.

It must be ten, there's no others.

Could we have missed one?

She looked behind them back down the stairs to where the women were. This is the one, Judy.

Fine.

The door was plain and cheap-looking, as if they could have punched through it. But it sat ajar. Deb stepped ahead of Judy and went inside.

Frank?

The flat was silent. The door opened into a living room and kitchen. There was no furniture to speak of, no kettle or toaster or TV, no curtains or blinds on the windows.

Da? Judy shouted. Her mother shushed her. To the side of the room was a shut door. There was a muffled tapping coming from the other side. It sounded in threes and fours, then stopped. They looked at one another and moved towards it.

Behind the door there was a short hallway and three more doors. Two of them were open. The third, in the opposite wall, was not. There were no windows in the hallway and the only light came through the open doors. They paused in the dim quiet until the tapping came again. From somewhere beyond the closed door it grew steadily louder and stopped again. They moved slowly forwards, past a clean white bathroom, an empty bedroom with a mirrored wardrobe, some tins of paint. They stopped. It was quiet again.

Frank, Deb said. She stepped forward and opened the door.

The room was empty. Only a box bed, mattressless, pushed against the far wall beneath a window. There was a seagull perched on the window ledge outside, stark white against slate roofs. It pecked the glass hard and the sound was loud in the little room. Judy stepped into the room and waved her arms, but it didn't move. She shouted and waved again. Then she went straight up to the window and slapped the glass. The seagull stood and stared into her face. It pecked the glass again.

*

When they went back downstairs the man was gone. There was still blood on the steps, a faint lingering scent of urine. Judy found his missing shoe on the landing below and left it balanced on the banister. There was no sound. The dim light felt heavy and they moved faster the closer they got to the ground floor.

On the way past the bin room Judy stopped and pointed at something in the dark. Deb squinted to make out the white number painted onto the side of a bin near the back wall, a number ten.

Let's go, Judy, she said.

Somewhere above them the singing started again, drifting down the stairs like smoke.

Nathaniel Cairney
IN WHICH TWO MAGPIES REALISE
THEY ARE NOT ALONE

Just when I'm certain it's not worth it
to write another word about birds,

there go two magpies bounding up and down
like Highland dancers surrounded by tarantulas,

their shiny dinosaur wings whipping outward
as if to say, *look how big I am, you worm-thieving bastard* –

at the window, I settle in to watch the fight.
I shift my weight, then lift my tea cup.

As bitter, then sweet, registers on my tongue,
the magpies scramble, panicked, toward the rising sun.

E. E. Chandler
THINGS YOU LEFT ME

For my father

A lifetime of diaries –
one detailing how you sat
with your father as he died
as I sat with you while you died,
notebook open on my lap.
Piles of notebooks –
one of party games
(although you never partied);
one of practical jokes;
one of long, bad jokes
like your long, dull stories –
about roadworks outside your window
or being stopped by police

and how you gave them what-for.
A love of words.
18 dictionaries in different languages –
French, German, Spanish, Greek and Hebrew.
9 books on conspiracy theories,
31 books on Space –
despite your belief that our planet
was only six thousand years old.
48 bibles, 1 in Doric.
1058 books about the bible.
Your old school jotters.
My old school jotters.
My old school art pads
with ungodly drawings
of kissing couples, a bare-chested man

and my naked self-portrait, aged fifteen,
which I hope you never saw.

Your album of cut-out pictures:
on one page, a pretty woman
in a bikini posing on rocks.
Overleaf,
the Virgin Mary posing on rocks,
eyes heavenward.
1 copy of *The Joy of Sex*
untouched
in its box buried at the back of your wardrobe.

A baby tooth in a matchbox
wrapped in cotton wool.
Another matchbox full of burnt matches.
An envelope full of the hair I cut off aged twelve –
those dark, glossy lengths
which broke your heart.
A tin of your bitten-off fingernails.

Stubbornness. Your temper.
The prominent family nose.
Your reticence with love.
Your words, which never leave me:
'You're a disappointment.'

Those memories of our last days together
in the Care Home.

You, an old man waking
from a young man's dream,
blowing kisses into the air.
Your mortified face when you realise
it's only the two of us here.

Rachel Clive
I MET YOUR SISTER TODAY

I met your sister today, now a full
Grown, care-worn mother, brimming with power.
We walked together through the Botanics,
Sheltered in the children's garden, between
Fruit trees and willow, drinking lemonade
From Lidl; I told her it was the place
You used to go, when you came to Glasgow.
I didn't know, she said. *I didn't know.*

I met your sister today, her man and
Their three children, on their way back to Wales
From Fort William. Her middle girl jiggled
With stories of hailstones striking her skin
Like missiles; the eldest collected cones
For a craft project, cradling them closely;
The youngest cartwheeled for the joy of it.
I thought I saw you in them, your spirit.

I met your sister in the Botanics.
I asked after you, I couldn't help it.
He's walking, even climbing trees again,
But I hardly ever see him. He's changed
Since the accident, since getting married.
She misses you. The children led us through
The glasshouses, from tropical to dry
Stroking cocoa plants and poking cacti.

In the Kibble the fish circled wishes
Deposited by hopeful visitors
Over the ages. Your sister's youngest

Reached up for my hand, held it softly in hers.
Time trembled in the trust of her touch. Words
Left us, could not do justice to the loss
Of what could have been, the love still denied.
The statues bore witness. Your sister smiled.

Claire Deans
GETTING RID OF GABRIELLA

Just as the two burly men started loading the boxes into the lorry, the rain, which had earlier been spitting, began coming down in sheets. Nicola told the men to come indoors until the downpour ended.

'You off to the Middle East then?' said the younger man. He was leaning against the living room wall, rolling his shoulders as if to relieve an ache. 'I've got a mate works out that way.'

'Is that right?' Nicola was distracted by Lara stomping up and down the wooden floorboards. She reached out as Lara passed and scooped her up onto her knee. 'Here. Have a biscuit, pet.'

'Loves it so he does.'

'Oh well that's good news,' said Nicola.

'Land of the sand, my mate calls it.'

'Seaside,' shouted Lara. 'Big big crabs,' and she made a pincer movement with her fingers, nipping Nicola's bare arm, dropping her biscuit onto the floor, wriggling to escape from the embrace.

'The wee one's full of energy,' said the older man. He slurped his tea.

Over by the patio doors, Lara was looking into a pram. She turned to face her audience. 'Awww no baba,' she sighed, shaking her head. She looked dejected. They all laughed and she scuttled to hide behind a box with the words *Seven Seas* printed on the side.

'Fancy pram that is,' said the younger man.

'It used to be Lara's.' Nicola picked up the biscuit from the floor. 'You can have the pram if you want. For free, of course.'

The man grinned. 'Well that's generous of you but I need to be finding myself a good woman first.'

'Oh, they're hard to find,' said the older man, laughing to reveal gaps between his teeth.

'It's an Italian design,' said Nicola, moving over to the pram. 'The model's called Gabriella. It's got an ergonomic seat, and all-terrain wheels.' She took hold of the handlebars. 'And – watch this.' She used her right hand to slide the catch. 'It's got one hand 3D compact folding.' She pushed her knee against the bassinet and the frame folded like a concertina. 'Voilà,' Nicola said, tucking the pram under her arm.

'You should be in sales, hen,' said the older man.

'Quack, quack,' said Lara, peeking out from behind a box.

The younger man pulled a funny face at her and she went back to hiding.

'Och, I just want someone to make good use of it,' Nicola said. 'It's such a great pram and in good condition.'

'Have you tried putting an ad up at Morrisons?' said the younger man.

'Aye. It's been there for weeks.'

'People have got too much these days,' said the older man, placing his cup on the floor.

*

Nicola had already phoned the girls to ask if they knew anyone who might need a pram. *Good luck, keep in touch, oh my god – you're so lucky!* None of them knew anyone.

The night before, she'd agreed to take it to the recycling centre. But as Frank had been lifting the pram out of the car boot its cover had caught on the edge. As if it was resisting, Nicola thought. She wondered if it was a message from her mum.

At general recycling the huge skip was filled to the brim. A one-wheeled child's tricycle, a broken bookshelf, smashed computer screens, an office chair, a burst sofa, a plywood sideboard, a rusty lawnmower, a pee-stained mattress, a bashed car door. It was a place of misery. Everything was dusty, rusted or decayed. All metal things mangled. From the surrounding trees, dead leaves and branches had been blown down by the wind, and were layered, shroud-like, on top.

Frank was about to hurl the pram into the skip when Nicola grabbed at his wrist. 'You can't do it.'

'What?'

'You can't get rid of Gabriella like this.'

He looked at her blankly. 'What do you mean?'

'Look,' she waved her arm towards the skip, her eyes filling. 'It's a graveyard of things.'

He sighed but placed the pram back on the ground. 'You've got an overactive imagination, Nic.'

Her tears began, unstoppable, and like faulty windscreen wipers her hands couldn't swipe them away fast enough. They were streaming down her cheeks, dripping from her chin.

'I can't believe you're this upset,' Frank said. 'It's just a pram.'

Images of her mum pushing the pram back and forth through those early endless nights of colic and teething had been pouring into her mind. 'Dickhead,' she had said, fiercely. 'It's more than a pram.'

*

Nicola typed out a quick message when they got to the top of the hill.

Hi Frank hope your last day is going good! The removal men have been and gone. Sorry again about last night and what I called you. Promise the pram will be gone by the time you get back xxx

A bell tinkled as they entered the charity shop. Over in the corner, the assistant was busy straightening a row of men's shirts. As they stood waiting at the counter, Nicola put up the hood of the pram, smoothing out any creases. Lara lifted a tartan pen from a box and began babbling to it.

Finally, the woman went behind the cash desk. 'Yes?' She shifted her glasses from her forehead to her nose.

'I want to donate—'

'I can't take it.' The woman was looking at the pram and shaking her head. 'Health and safety regulations.'

'But it's completely safe. It's practically brand new.'

'Health and safety.'

'It's from Baby World.'

And as if it were only yesterday, Nicola saw herself wandering up and down the long rows of prams, buggies and strollers. She remembered the moment when she had spotted Gabriella. The canopy had the silver-grey colour and lustre of armour. It looked sturdy and invincible. A warrior in the pram range. The hefty price tag was attached to the handle bar with a loop made from tiny steel balls like cannonballs.

They had read through the long list of specifications. 'What does *Aerodynamic Wheels* mean?' her mum had asked.

'I think it means it can fly,' Nicola smiled, folding and unfolding the *All-Inclusive Canopy*, pressing the heel of her hand into the *Large, Ultra-Padded Ergonomic Seat*.

'Let me buy it for you, Nicola. I've been putting money away every week,' said her mum. 'From the cleaning. It's amazing how quickly it adds up.'

And Nicola knew the sacrifices that would have been made. The shift from Tesco to Lidl, no luxury buys or treats. The notes would have been hidden below her mum's underwear in the chest of drawers. She had always been suspicious of banks, intimidated by orderly queues and hushed voices, the professional lipsticked smile of the teller.

'It's far too much, Mum,' Nicola had said.

'I'm paying for it, Nicola. No arguments.' She had pulled out a bulky envelope from her handbag and was marching towards the cash desk.

Even baby Lara had kicked at her ribs as if siding with her soon-to-be granny.

Nicola was pulled back to the present. The woman was telling Lara to put the pen back in the box.

'My mum loved going for walks along the Nith with that pram,' said Nicola, easing the pen out from Lara's grasp.

'Health and safety,' the woman repeated like an automaton.

An elderly man looked up from a book he was reading. 'Health and safety gone mad,' he said, shaking his head.

The woman narrowed her eyes. 'It's the rules. I don't make them.'

*

Outside the charity shop, the wind was ice cold. Nicola buttoned up Lara's eskimo hood. For the love of Jesus, surely someone must want the pram. 'You know,' she said to Lara, 'your granny used to drive down from Glasgow every week and push you in that pram.'

'Lara's pram,' she said, 'Mummy push Lara.'

'You're too big, Lara,' said Nicola. 'Lara's a big girl now.'

'Mummy push Lara,' she growled, clutching the metal frame.

'No. Lara's too big.'

Lara came to a halt, folded her arms, stuck out her bottom lip.

Choose your battles carefully.

A few minutes later, Nicola was pulling the harness to its longest length and strapping it around Lara's shoulders and waist. Squashed into the bassinet she looked like a giant, rosy cheeked doll.

'Fast,' Lara demanded, 'fast.' Her glassy blue eyes were full of mischief.

'Hold on to the sides, pet,' said Nicola, marvelling how the wheels were gliding over the cobblestones. Bobbing up and down on the large seat, Lara was giggling wildly. Outside the bakers a woman with a walking stick smiled.

'Faster Mummy,' Lara shouted, 'faster.' By the job centre and the new craft ale pub where a springer spaniel barked and strained its leash. A lad on a bike passed them by and tinkled his bell.

At the bottom of the hill Nicola slowed down and pushed the pram across the road to the river. 'That was fun, wasn't it my darling?' she said. 'Do you want to see the birdies?'

She gripped onto Lara as they leaned over the stone wall of the
river bank to see the water cascading over the weir and the seagulls
lined haphazardly across the top. There was no-one else around
and impulsively Nicola shouted, 'Health and safety, my arse.'

The words were whipped off by the strong wind. She imagined
them strung together like the alphabet banner in Lara's bedroom,
heading down towards the bend in the river, before reaching high
tide at the Solway Coast.

'My arse,' Lara said, smiling sweetly. Nicola heard her mum's
chuckle. 'Arse, arse, arse,' chimed Lara.

'Look, Lara,' said Nicola pointing to a large seagull whose wings
were stretched for takeoff. 'Where do you think it's going to fly?'

'Seaside,' said Lara. 'See crabs.'

The distraction technique. Another from her mum's bag of tricks.

*

Walking along their street, Nicola saw a red Volvo parked in a
driveway. The new neighbours. The woman was expecting.

'I just want to talk to this lady for a wee bit,' said Nicola. She
rang the doorbell. From inside, there began high-pitched barking.
'Doggie,' said Lara.

Footsteps came thumping down the hall and the yapping
increased.

'Hi,' Nicola said. The woman was holding a toy poodle. Its rusty
hair had been styled into a bouffant. 'I'm sorry I haven't introduced
myself before—'

'Shut up Cherry,' snapped the woman to the dog.

Nicola nodded at the woman's bump. 'I don't know if you have
a pram yet?'

She batted her long eyelashes. 'My husband is ordering me one.
A Mothercare Silvercross.' Cherry began whining and she cuffed
the dog across its head. 'Sshh.'

'You can have this one,' Nicola said, wheeling Gabriella forward.
'It's a great pram. I don't want anything for it.'

The woman glanced at the pram. 'I like things *new*,' she said. 'This one's as good as new.'

'*Brand* new.' The woman began to close the door. 'I've something on the stove.'

'Thanks then,' said Nicola to the wooden door.

If that was how she treated the yapping dog, Nicola wondered how she would cope with a newborn baby screeching throughout the night. She could remember the intense demands of the early days. On one side Lara would be mewling, latching, sucking greedily, and on the other, Frank pressed hard against her rump. She had felt that her body no longer belonged to her, that it had become an involuntary donation for the pleasure of others.

As they crossed the road they met the postwoman walking down the drive.

She glanced inside the pram. 'I thought you'd had another one there, Nic. I thought to myself have I blinked and missed something.'

Nicola laughed. 'You must be joking. One's enough as it is.'

*

Halfway through the Disney film, Lara's body became heavier, one arm dropping off the edge of the sofa. Nicola watched the ebb and flow of her chest and felt the warmth in her oceanic breaths. Then, as if Lara were dreaming of the breast, the tip of her tongue flicked through her funnelled mouth. She was drooling. Deep inside there still existed remnants of the baby.

But was one enough? The question seemed to come out of nowhere and startled Nicola. *Of course, it was. One was enough, wasn't it?*

Her mum's ability to settle baby Lara with her soft melodic singing seemed almost mystical. With her rendition of the Skye Boat Song, the baby's eyes would become heavy-lidded. Halfway through Coorie Doon her tense limbs would limpen. At the second verse of Fields of Athenry the baby's heavy head was already nestled in the crook of her mum's shoulder. Her mum would finish singing the ballad before gently laying baby Lara in the Moses basket.

Yet Nicola, weakened from blood loss and surgery, had dreaded each day anew. You cow, she told herself, you slow snivelling fat cow. She couldn't find enough adjectives for her failure.

Her mum had given up her cleaning job and began driving up weekly from Glasgow.

*

After putting Lara to bed, Nicola went out into the back garden and sat on the loveseat where she used to drink spritzers with her mum on light summery evenings. She shivered, zipping up her puffer jacket against the chill of the evening.

Then she closed her eyes and inhabited the body of her mum, replaying each stage of the journey through her eyes.

Looming high on the hills the turbine blades are slowly circling as if threatening decapitation. When the mist falls she drops a gear and switches to full beam. The road is bereft of vehicles and glitters sharply with hoar frost.

On a barren stretch of road a sign shows a flag flapping. Strong winds begin to jostle the small car as if it is a plaything for the heavens. She grips the steering wheel tighter. Her hands break out in sweat. Her breathing becomes irregular.

Cat's eyes have lit up a pathway of enchantment towards junction 27 and her breath steadies. She begins listening to the top twenty Christmas songs countdown.

Trees line the highway. Their spindly claw-branches begin to oscillate. Clouds congregate. Then the heavens open and rain comes battering down, icy rain flooding the windscreen so the frantic wipers won't wipe fast enough. There begins her own internal tempest. Hammering heart, panting breath, sweating palms, trembling. Loss of control.

She freezes.

Frank had said that the reason why she was late was because of the car. You couldn't trust an Austin Metro.

But why doesn't she answer her phone? Nicola had asked. You know what your mum's like with the mobile Nicola – you told me last week that she keeps forgetting how to use it. This was true. Plus, she had water retention resulting in swollen fingers. She had difficulty tapping the digits. It all made sense. Nicola had wanted it to make sense.

When the funeral director recommended a closed casket Nicola thought of her mum's limbs mutilated. Her kind freckled face fractured as a Picasso painting.

There had been a red weather warning alert. *Why don't you come down tomorrow instead? Nicola hadn't suggested.*

After enduring the evening's customary torment, Nicola wiped away her tears with the back of her hands.

She was about to turn and go indoors when she heard the hubbub. Although she could not yet see the birds she could hear their yelping, babbling, murmuring, yapping, barking, honking. The euphoric noise built to a crescendo as the skein of barnacle geese began to come into view. Then they were there. Above her. Their faces flashing white in the dusk. Their V formation etched against the sky.

She felt suddenly elated thinking of their spectacular journey from the arctic circle. V for Victory. The geese tourists were flying towards the wild saltmarshes and sandbanks at the estuary. Nicola envied them for their certainty of direction. The compass inside their small poised heads. She watched them until they disappeared, then she turned off the patio light and went indoors.

But was one enough? The voice in her head had returned again demanding an answer. For a few seconds she looked intently at the pram in the corner. Then she folded it. She placed it next to the suitcases.

Upstairs, she undressed to shower and stood in front of the bedroom mirror. She examined the scar across her belly. An emergency exit from her uncooperative body. Once it had been inflamed and oozing fluid. It had long healed, fading to a silvery delicate marking. An indelible imprint of the life she had brought into the world.

Lara Delmage
CRUSH

Sucks the flesh off
the olive pit
of my stomach
Thumbs my head
first deep
into arid soil &
returns me
Waters
break me &
spits
for good measure &
chants
Smut smut smut
But!
Crushed
in the mineral gloam
I fantasise silver-green leaves
tumultuous branches
oily fruits that'll
hang wanton
off my many arms &
hands that'll pick me
wanting &
chant back
I must! I must! I must!

I DON'T CRY

When I'm upset
my armpits grow wet
I piss
every five minutes
I sweat
even
between my toes
Ladies, *hello*, that's why my skin glows!
did you know that tears get more acidic
as the day goes
why in the evening
I bathe (lactose intolerant) in milk
and pickle myself
in fat
chip away at the barnacles
sucking at the salt
in my pore pools
with a chisel
and come out
a statue

Johana Egermayer
ÀITE NAN IOMADH LOCH

'. . . gun ach ainmean sgrìobhte marbh
air a' chloinn 's na fir 's na mnathan
a chuir Rèanaidh às an fhearann
eadar ceann a tuath na Creige
's an Caisteal a thogadh do MhacSuain
no do Mhac Ghille Chaluim
airson fòirneart agus dìon.'
                    —'Sgreapadal', Somhairle MacGill-Eain

'. . . 's an dèidh sin, an dèidh sin,
tha mi gu bhith 'na mo charragh-cuimhne.'
                    —'Ged a Thillinn A-nis', An Rathad Cian,
                              Ruaraidh MacThòmais

I: Losgadh na Tìre
Teine a' strì ri uisge tro na linntean.
An loch a bh' ann an toiseach.
Staidhre sa ghàrradh, agus co-shìnte rithe
dà allt a' ruith san amaran de ghaineamh-chlach.

Chaidh an taigh-mòr na smàl
uair ro thric thairis air ùine.
Dèan peanas no mallachd dheth.
No tubaist. Do roghainn-sa.

An dèidh a bhith a' gluasad eaglaisean,
– am mìorbhail sin,
tunnaichean is tunnaichean
de chlach shnaidhte, ainglean, agus airsean,
air an tarraing airson naoi ceud slat,
fhad 's a bha an saoghal air fad a' coimhead,

air a bheò-glacadh, is aig an aon àm
an seann bhaile a' dol an deachamh
le daineamait –

chan eil e buileach cho doirbh
a bhith a' gluasad dhaoine.

Fhuair iad ionadan an àite taighean,
ann an cathair bhàn a chaidh a thogail,
ri taobh làrach a' chomhaltaich
air an robh an dearbh ainm,
mearachadh-sùla concrait air a' chnoc,
a' cumail faire ris an uaigh staoin.

Dh'fhalbh an loch,
is chaidh an tìr air fad na lasadh,
ìobairt-loisgte air leac teasa.

Saighdearan fo mhisg mun cuairt teine-èibhinn
a rinn iad le leabhraichean is spùinn na seilg'.
Roimhe seo, leagh iad deiseachan-cruaidhe
agus clogaidean airson spòrs.

Nach iongantach gu bheil
mèinn-uachdair gu math coltach ri loch,
ach falamh, sin an rud. Tioram.

II: Na h-Ìomhaighean Àileach

Ach roimhe seo, bha tuathanaich ann,
a' solarachadh rìomhadh is sàimh
an taigh-mhòir, àrd air sliabh na beinne.
Bailtean sgiobalta, achaidhean torrach,
ceòl is cuideachd, sealg is seinn.
Òr-mheasan agus fìgean ag abachadh
ann an teas nan taighean-glainne,
ainmhidhean bho thìrean cèin
a' dol ànrach anns a' bhuaile,
cinn-cloiche nam mòr-rìghrean Ròmanach
a' coimhead suas bhon bhalla le plìon.
Le belle immagini.

An oighreachd gu lèir air a dealbhachadh
mar ghàrradh gàirdeachais,
ach le prothaid fhallain a' tighinn gun sgur
bho na raointean – agus bho na mèinnean,
oir bha iadsan ann mar-thà:
Èibhlean an sgriosa a bha fhathast ri teachd.
Ho con me l'inferno mio.

Am balach seo a thogadh
eadar an taigh-mòr is na seann choilltean,
theich e gu Pràg an toiseach.
An dèidh sinn thàinig Eadailt, Sasainn, fiù 's an Ruis.
Cò aig a tha fios ma bha seanais nan craobhan-faidhbhile
fhathast a' cagair na chluasan.
No glaodh nan slocaichean, mar ro-chluich.
Ach 's iongantach gun robh. Bha cus ciùil eile ann.
Dell'aure il susurrar, il mormorar de rivi.

A-nis, tha com a' chù de chlach
na laighe san duslach air an làr,
taobh ri innealan àiteachais air aimhreit,
iarann toinnte air a chòmhdach le meirg,
agus spealgan uigh liath bhreac.
Stad fiù 's an sealg thaibhseil.
Fàileadh lus na tùise,
aghaidh-thogalaich air a rùsgadh
mar chraiceann bolgach anns a' ghrèin.
Che puro ciel, che chiaro sol!

Tha e buaireil
a bhith ag èisteachd ri criomagan ciùil
am measg duslach, eòrnach, agus sgrios
ann an tobhta an talla-cluiche.
Chan fhaigh thu ach balbhachd ghramail.
La quiete che qui tanto regna.

Orfeo a threòraich Euridice
à tìr nam marbh,
ach thionndaidh e.
'S e rud cunnartach
a th' ann an sealladh air ais,
oir ann am priobadh na sùla
bidh an taigh-mòr, na coilltean,
na bailtean, na h-achaidhean,
a h-uile càil a' teicheadh ann an toit.
Ombre sdegnose, deh, placatevi con me.

Che farò, dove andrò?
Tha mi gu bhith na mo stalla-guail.

III: Caoineadh is Cagar

'Nuair a bha sinn òg,
b' àbhaist dhuinn a bhith a' suirghe
air bàtaichean beaga air an loch
ann am meadhan a' bhaile.'

'Tha cuimhne agam fhathast
càit' an robh taigh mo cho-ogha,
ach dh'fhalbh na cuid eile bhuam.'

Chualas nuallan is blaodhan cruidh
a chaidh fhàgail anns na bailtean.
An dèidh beagan làithean, thàinig tost.
Na b' ainmiche, donnalaich nam faol-daoine.

'Am feasgar mu dheireadh
a chuir sinn seachad aig an taigh,
bha an dealan dheth.
Cha robh ach lampa-eòlain againn air a' bhòrd,
am baile a-mach à sealladh mar-thà, mar gum b' eadh.
Dh'fhalbh sinn sa mhadainn, is cha do thill sinn tuilleadh.
Cha robh dad air fhàgail. Chuir iad an solas às.'

Ulbersdorf, Kommern, Bartelsdorf,
Neudorf, Niedergeorgenthal.
Na h-ainmean a' tàisleachadh
mar chagairean fiatach air uachdar an locha –
is cò seo a tha ag èisteachd riutha?
Chan eil duine ann.

IV: Ròs-chraobhan is Eòrna

Chaidh am fearann thionndadh
gu achaidhean-guail
– ach, achaidhean co-dhiù –
agus bha foghar ann, dubh is teth,
a' tighinn bho na raointean
a chaidh sgrìobadh às
mar chraiceann is feòil
gus cothrom fhaighinn air na cnàmhan.
Àm gu curachd, àm gu buain.

Dè bhios a' tighinn às an talamh a-nis?
Ròs-chraobhan bho ghàrradh-uchdain,
a' lunnadh air na seann choilltean-faidhbhile.
Duilleagan mèith, dìleagan caithteach,
ùr, bras, coigreach – ach 's e fàs a th' ann.

Agus air bruaichean nan lochan ùra
tha craobhan, preasan, lusan
a thàinig gun iarraidh, gun sireadh.
Chan eil iad sgiobalta no snasail,
na tuinichean stèidheachail seo,
ach tha iad deònach ath-shìolachadh,
agus teicheadh a chur air an eòrna taibhseach
a b' àbhaist a bhith a' gasadh
bho na h-achaidhean fàs.

V: Loch os cionn an Locha
Ach a dh'aindheoin abachadh toite is teasa,
dhrùidh uisge air ais, mean air mhean.
Buaidh na fliche.

Tha na lochan ùra a' lìonadh suas,
na mèinnean air an sgioladh,
falamh, caithte, gun fheum,
gual gu lèir air a thoirt a-mach.
Uisge a' tighinn agus a' cur am falach
gach toll is gach sloc.
Ann am bliadhna no dhà,
bidh luchd-turais a' snàmh ann,
agus ag iomradh air longan-toileachais.

Bha loch ann an toiseach,
agus mairidh na lochan.
Agus mur am bi an loch seo,
bidh lochan eile ann.

Chaidh Caisteal Eisenberg / Jezeří a thogail anns na Beanntan Mèinne
(Erzgebirge) eadar a' Ghearmailt agus an t-Seic anns an 14mh linn. Eadar
an 18mh agus an 19mh linn, b' e ionad cultarail cudromach aig ìre eadar-
nàiseanta a bh' ann, agus bha ceanglaichean làidir aig co-ghleusaichean
leithid Gluck (a thogadh air an oighreachd), Haydn, agus Beethoven
ri Eisenberg. Aig àm an dàrna cogaidh, b' e prìosan Nàsach a bh' ann.
Anns na 1960an agus 1970an, chaidh na bailtean mun cuairt a' chaisteil

44

fhuadachadh agus sgriosadh gu tur air sgàth mèinnearachd ghuail. Mhair an caisteal air iomall na talmhainn fhàs seo. Anns an latha a th' ann, bidh na seann mhèinnean gu tric a' dol fon uisge, mar phàirt de leasachadh na h-àrainneachd.

Criomagan bho na h-oparan le Gluck, Paride ed Elena *agus* Orfeo ed Euridice:

Le belle immagini = Na h-ìomhaighean / na cuimhneachan àileach

Ho con me l'inferno mio = 'S ann còmhla rium a tha m' ifrinn-sa

Dell'aure il susurrar, il mormorar de rivi = Cagar nan gaothan, torman nan allt

Che puro ciel, che chiaro sol! = Adhar cho glan, grian cho geal!

La quiete che qui tanto regna = An t-sàmhchair a tha a' rìoghachadh an seo gu mòr

Ombre sdegnose, deh, placatevi con me = Sibhse, a sgàthan goiceile, ò, sìthichibh leam

Che farò, dove andrò? = Dè nì mi, càit' 'n tèid mi?

Graham Fulton
DO YOU FEEL

the sound at the back of your throat
do you feel the sound at the back of your throat
do you feel the sound at the back of your throat

do you feel the sound at the back of your throat
do you feel the sound of something to say
do you feel the sound of something to say
at the back of your throat

do you feel the sound of the back of your throat
do you feel the shape of a sound
do you feel the shape of a sound
do you feel a shape of the sound
do you feel the sound of a shape
at the back of your throat
the back of your thought

do you feel your thought at the back of the sound
do you feel the thought at the back of your sound
do you feel the thought at the back of your sound

do you feel the thought at the back of your throat
do you think you know what you want
do you think you remember the birth
do you think you make it happen
do you feel the sound at the back of your throat
do you think you know what you want
do you think you remember the seed
do you think you remember the opening
do you think you remember the birth

do you think you remember the opening up
do you think you make it happen

do you feel the sound
on the back of your throat
do you feel the seed at the back of your throat
do you feel the sound of something to say
do you feel the sound of something to say
do you feel a sound of something to say
do you feel the seed of something to think
do you think you need
to have something to say

do you feel the sound at the back of your throat
do you feel the sound of something to say
at the back of your thought
do you think you make it happen
do you think we can stop whenever we want?

Niamh Gordon
FOOD

The baby is born. The woman gives birth to the baby, a gift which involves torn flesh and shock and blood splashed on the skirting board. The baby is grey first, then purple, then pink and finally puce and screaming, a joyful sound because it means the baby's aquatic lungs have coughed up all their mucus and water and welcomed in the air. The baby is connected to the inside of the woman by a gnarled grey cord full of blood. They wait for the blood to drain. The afterbirth comes suddenly, and then the baby is no longer connected to the woman but to this large meat object, an organ grown and now discarded.

The cord drains and they cut through it. Baby loose in the world. They stitch the torn flesh of the woman with a needle and thread as though her flesh were fabric, but it is not fabric. It is skin and nerves. Apparently she has been given anaesthetic, delivered with what they called a scratch but what felt to her like fire. The anaesthetic is not touching the sides. In and out the needle goes, pulling through the ripped skin and she gapes with the pain. The baby whimpers and attempts to latch.

There is food being made in her body, food for the baby, coming from her breast. The baby knows to find the food, writhing and mouthing, but this instinct does not mean it is easy for the baby to feed. The baby attempts again to latch and the woman swears. This does not make sense to her. The purest image: babe at breast, mother iconolatry. Yet the baby is fussing and crying, and the latch is wrong, and her nipples are blistering already.

The afterbirth has been whisked away. Days later she feels sad about this. What happened to it, this organ that she made? This heap of meat that came out of her body and was taken? She never really looked at it, she would have liked to marvel at her creation and to thank it for its work. She reads online that some women plant it in their gardens, let it nourish the soil. That would have been nice, to grow more life from this life-giver. She asks the midwife at one of the follow-up appointments. The midwife says, oh that, it's medical waste. What do they do with medical waste? They burn it.

*

She reads lots online in the next few days. She holds her phone close to her face and lets the blue light spill into her skull, willing it to keep her awake as the baby sucks at her breast. She glimpses sleep in between feeds. Her eyes roll with the fatigue. It is two a.m. Tiredness is not the word, this is something deeper. Other. It is two forty-five. She is drained. It is three ten. Her body, her face, it all aches. It is three thirty. She's ravenous, she kicks her husband to try and wake him, please, a slice of toast, anything. It is four thirty (a whole hour!). She drinks so much water it makes her feel sick. It is five oh five. It is five thirty-seven.

The baby has figured out the feeding thing and her gratitude is total. They worked on it together. Nose to nipple. Tilt the head back. No, too shallow a latch. Try again. She weeps, she yells, she thrusts the baby at his well-meaning face and says, well you fucking do it then. The night her milk comes in she can literally see her breasts solidify in front of her, they are bruised concrete and she has a new blister on her nipple which scabs and tears open again and again and she cries and cries and cries. Then, the baby can suddenly do it. Like he always knew how and was just testing her.

*

Five thirty-seven, again. She has begun to feel fond of it, of that arrangement of numbers on her phone. She sees five thirty-seven every morning and it is like a friend, a promise that they've nearly made it through. She yawns. She has not slept for more than twenty minutes at a time this night. She keeps falling asleep with the baby on her chest, which isn't safe but she can't stay awake. Eyes rolling, sleep swamping over her. Gasping awake as he mewls for her, for her milk.

The baby is asleep now, though. She is able to place him down in his crib at the side of the bed and slide her arm out from underneath him and he hardly stirs. This feels like the punchline to something.

She stands, stretches, makes her way downstairs, moves through the air silently. She, a dawn ghost. She goes into the garden. It is grey and quiet out, the sun not yet risen. She steps onto the lawn which has grown wild for lack of mowing. Tall grasses have seeded and weeds have sprung up between them. They tickle her calves. Her bare feet are cold and wet now. She kneels, pauses, and then pushes her face into the damp ground.

She is tender. Her tear has not yet healed. The doctor says this is normal. Normal to be raw like this? Normal to be in pieces? In the bathroom she uses a hand mirror and puts one leg up on the toilet seat. She doesn't recognise what she sees. Cannot even see the stitches submerged within shapes that make no sense. She begins to question her own anatomy, the anatomy of all bodies that have birthed a baby. Does everyone look like this? Everything is swollen out of shape, distorted and mangled. Grey. Puce.

*

Five thirty-seven again. Was it a better night? She yawns. At first she was using an app to mark the sleeps and the wakings and the feeds but the numbers were both abstract and depressing. Now she prefers to forget. The baby in the crib is slumbering. She goes downstairs, outside. It rained all night, the soundtrack to what little sleep she managed was the hiss of water running down gutters. She lies on the grass on her back so that she is facing the grey sky. She claws her hands into the lawn. Grinds her fingers down into the soil. Slime and grit. She wipes soil on her face with one hand, then the other.

Inside she uses a wet tea-towel to scrub the dirt off her skin. She catches a glimpse of herself reflected in the greasy oven. The dirt has left a trace.

*

The joy is fierce and wracks her body just the same as the grief, the shock, the pain. She feels demolished by it. When the baby opens his eyes, when he makes a gassy smile. When he squeaks in his sleep and she thinks, a dream? Already? A whole world inside that head, one she will only ever know parts of. She weeps, with joy and with something else which she cannot name but sees in the eyes of the other mothers at the church playgroup. Rage, or fear, or both. A hunger.

Five thirty-seven. She yawns. The baby twitches in his sleep. He frowns, then smiles, then frowns again, like a robot practicing pre-programmed facial expressions. Outside it is cooler than yesterday. The rain has not abated and the mud is wet and claggy. She takes handfuls and rubs it into her face and hair, then her neck and her forearms and her shins. She digs. She tastes the mud. It is mineral and sour. She has read online that some women crave soil when they are pregnant. They want to eat it because of a nutrient deficiency. Poor them, she thinks. The baby a parasite sapping them of everything, driving them to dig in the garden just so they can satiate themselves. The gnarled cord draining. Lifeforce. She feels a small pebble between her teeth and bites down. There's a crack.

In the shower she rinses the mud away and feels bereft.

*

The emergency dentist agrees to see her, for no small fee. She thought postpartum it would be free? Not for emergencies. She offers her open mouth and they stab and poke with sharp instruments. Cracked a molar. Not much you can do. It costs a lot of money and it hurts.

Five thirty-seven, and there are birds singing this time. It didn't rain last night and the mud is more compacted. She can see the holes she has made in the lawn. They don't look like molehills, she thinks. Can't say it was moles. Maybe a fox, a vixen building a den for her cubs. The mud tastes different today, saltier. She has eaten several worms, they are bitter and wet. The salt could be from a different kind of animal. Sweat or urine or something else, soaking into the ground. The more she chews and swallows, the calmer she feels. So calm she could just about drift off, lying here on the lawn on her side, buried in the weeds and grasses and dirt. Then her milk lets down, wet patches blooming across her chest and she can hear, on some frequency that is not audible to most, the sudden yelp of her baby waking and knowing that she is not there. She runs back inside. Mud trodden into the carpet, smeared on the wallpaper. Takes her baby in her arms. He is screaming by this point, face screwed up, mouthing around for her breast, for her. Her fingers are smeared with dirt but her nipple is clean. He latches. They both sigh.

She won't leave him again like that. Alone in the world and screaming out for food. Tomorrow, she will take him outside with her and show him the beauty of the earth. Tomorrow, they can taste the mud together.

Zoë Green
LEVEN STREET

acrylic carpet in a rented room, its windows
smeared with rain and dust from buses squeezing past
the betting shop, the chippie, the Londis

a notice pinned to the door that says *your turn to mop*
the stairs that smell of bleach and pitiless stone
that turn

      and turn

            on themselves

      corkscrews

            going nowhere

      that echo yet

      you did not make

            a sound

    he lives here now

            and

there are

    1. books by the bed that have no pictures

    2. pictures by the bed of a woman's rudeness engraved

Rented. Divorced. Child support. Joint custody. We love you.
We just don't love each other (anymore).

my mother is a visitor who sleeps beneath the herringbone rug;
I in the slant-space beneath his drawing board
where I ping the wires vibrating
the charred silence between them
everything is zigzags

                          diagonals
                                    cross-hatching

                                              *dis*sonance
Not like the rolling hills of home,
These sunset songs o' mauve
That swallow Angus's purple loam,
Their bedroom's sacred grove;
Now their leid's fallen out of tune –
They've lost their tongue and groove.

(though none of this idea of unity was ever entirely true because
the bedroom with its tongue and groove was a dark, unhappy place
where branches tapped the window as my mother lay dying and
my father was, through no fault of his own, obliged to live in a
faraway city with another family)

Lydia Harris
ROBERT DICK
baker/botanist of Thurso

his mother

1

she died shortly after the hazelnuts were ripe giving birth,
she gathered wild geraniums, she cannot shake them off
shortly after she died she broke a twig with some of the
blossom giving birth to her fourth child, she shrinks from
the world shortly after giving birth she died

2

she swept strips of dough to the bakehouse floor her
country vanished through the mists he could see her at the
hill-foot tempting him to dream, alive unable to cross the
burn, he should like to see her once more, stooping low to
the ground he turned round found butterworts in scores

3

the land is the shape of her absence, he walks over it dressed
in a long coat of roses and peat, he walks into the land and it
sighs around him so do the grasses along the river, the
mosses on the boulders, he walks into the land on the
morning of a wraith, it forms around him the shape of her
absence

4

when murk rolled from the hill patting the window with
moth wings, he called to her, his annals were filled with her,
his records of moss, how it nourished its dead year after year,
he heard her voice float under ancient alder and willow, he
walked home in his hairy rillens fastened at the calf with
bone toggles

5

a list appears in his oil cloth pocket book, she haunts the
margin of each page, he doesn't find her well, yearns for her
face to shine, sphagnum teaches him to lay down his life for
hers, bitter vetch the list goes, purging flax, hemlock and
though he hasn't seen them, adds starry mosses, sweet
vernal grass

6

he tells the rock dove in the kailyard, seven loaves crouch in
my window, the brown blankets curl on my bed, listen
replies the blue green flame of the dove, step into my throat,
my eyes are skylights, my muscles tracks, the click click of
my bones will steady your steps

Benjamin K. Herrington
YO' MOMMA

yo' momma
ain't never liked ur boyfriends
not a one
fo' sho' she ain't like me
she's envious
brittle bones
venomous marrow

yo' momma
always wanted u to live her dreams
bind u up in her old traditions
imprison u in moldy towers
she ain't never forgave herself
not yo' daddy, not no one else
for tradin' River Forth
for the mighty Mississipp'

yo' momma
she ain't realise
my momma's momma
spoke with spirits too
my momma's momma
drank Coors Light
out silver cans like silver bullets
she wasn't 'bout to let no old world spirits
fuck with me

new world spirits
tol' my momma's momma
i was comin'
long before i arrived
they saw me fly
thru Callanish stones
thru St Louis Arch
on my way to be reborn

real real early one morning
before i could tell any stories
sing any songs
i went to wake my momma's momma
pullin' up on her eyelids
as dawn broke
down the windows

my momma's momma
wasn't sleepin' or awake
eyeballs white clouds
full of spirits
that's when i knew
this blue-eyed boy
fenna cheat death
more than once

& how mr. death like me now
he don't
like yo' momma
he don't at all

but when i tell stories
death cup his ear
when i sing songs
death dance
like how i run
flyin' over them jagged rocks
at the edge of Lake Michigan
giddy gleeful grinnin'
dead ass
i'm still alive

yo' daddy
was a giant
Midwest born & raised
u tol' me once
how yo' momma's lil' brother
would throw rocks at yo' daddy
when he'd come a courtin'
up to the Highlands
after yo' daddy was done playin' ball
after he was done dunkin' on all them
red-faced wee & angry Scots

yo' momma's momma
laughed & laughed
with yo' momma & her sisters
yo' daddy coulda got angry
he was tall
but he was playin' small
in order to win

u got the magick in u
i felt it real good
first time we went to bed
in ur bedroom
in yo' momma's ivy-covered house
in our old neighborhood
in St Louis
i knew trouble brewin'
but damn
i liked it

u even wrote a poem
a warnin'
typed it out
on yellow paper
framed it in a vintage frame
put it on ur vanity
right beneath the mirror

what ur poem say
somethin' like
u a crème brulee
sharp edges outside
soft & creamy inside
'take your time', u wrote
'the pleasure's all mine'

i spent endless days & nights
between ur lovely legs
lookin' up into heaven
i ate ur groceries from behind
u moant into ur pillow
while i squeezed ur lemonlimes
u was lookin' at me glowin'
green eyes open'd wide
the pleasure was all mine

i still dream
of ur damp heather
i still miss u
sleepin' on my chest
loungin' languorously
ur leg over me
while we torpid on the couch
watchin' PBS specials
or BBC news

u ever ask yo' self why
we kept meetin' up
over & over & over &
why we kept runnin' 'round the world &
why u ain't never
just run away
with me

some nights i know
u still visitin' me
half-moon princess
peepin' thru my windows
watchin' in my dreams
u ever hear me howlin' by the river
u remember now
my name

u remember how you tol' me once
yo' momma's momma tol' u once
'what's comin' to ye won't pass ye bye'
well all righty then
it don't matter if yo' momma liked me
it don't matter if u stuck up for me

my momma &
my momma's momma
they gone on ahead
tho' they still be whisperin' in my ear
they tol' me to sing u this old song
in my new words
c'mon now
hear me out

in them old Caledonian forests
yo' momma's growlin' coorse
over a darkened 'bervie loch
she's hurlin' bullet staines
in cold winds full o' fury
blowin' off them Hebrides
yo' momma's roarin' ain't but noise
yo' momma can't say shite to me

when ur beauty thaws like springtime
when we's smellin' petrichor
spirits float thru Evanston gardens
sunlight shines Lake Michigan shores
whole world grows green to heaven
when i sing these ancient songs
i only see u now in dreams
where i still hold u in my arms

when i tell tales 'bout us
my hotcold princess
u best believe we never lose
we only win &
i'm tellin' u once more
my love
don't never forget
i'll always b ur Huckleberry

–fin–

Michael Hopcroft
ECHOES FROM CALDER GLEN

Garrat's Linn

Around two hundred metres north of Ravenscraig a well-defined track leads to a remarkably deep and wide pool in the Calder traditionally known as *Garrat's Linn* but better known by locals today as *The Gurrets*. Reputed in olden times to be 'bottomless', this pool can be measured today at over nine metres (or around thirty feet) in depth: more than the height of a two-storey building.

The name Garrat's Linn – first recorded in the nineteenth century, but likely much older – appears to have a Scots etymology: *garrat* translating as a turret or watch tower, and seemingly referring to the prominent crag which stands over the pool and is a popular jumping-in point for thrill-seekers today. *Linn*, meanwhile, is a Scots word which can mean either a waterfall or a pool in a river. In this instance it denotes only the latter. At Garrat's Linn there is no waterfall to speak of: the deep pool, instead, sits below a sequence of rapids, a run of the river which, for summer visitors, may have the appearance of a mere wimpling brook, but when in spate becomes a foaming frenzy. The state of agitation of the water, for those who have not witnessed it, can perhaps best be imagined by considering that it is this action, and this action alone, which has scoured Garrat's Linn to such a remarkable depth, and continues to keep it clear of deposits and accumulation today.

In consequence of its remarkable depth and width Garrat's Linn is amongst the most well-adapted sites in the Calder for outdoor swimming. It is also amongst the most popular. On warm summer days it is not uncommon to find people (both locals and visitors from further afield) bathing here. In doing so they are continuing a tradition that has been in existence for centuries, if not millennia. As early as the 1860s, reference may be found to *Garrat's Linn*, as well as to another less conspicuous pool in the Calder around five hundred metres further upstream known as *Sandy Linn*, being 'much frequented by bathers during the Summer time'. And the popularity of these two favoured bathing spots is perhaps even more clearly evidenced by the depiction in the first edition Ordnance Survey map of 1858 of a well-defined footpath extending all the way from the village of Lochwinnoch, through the woods of the glen, to the very banks of these linns.

Today, only parts of these once well-defined footpaths remain discernible: kept alive, where they have been, by continued, sporadic use across the centuries. In the places where they do survive, hollowed deep into the ground, these tracks hold the footprints of generations. Desire lines, written into the landscape by countless weavers, mill-workers, laundry girls and inestimable others in the period since, who all sought the cold and invigorating waters of the Calder, they tell, perhaps more evocatively than any prose, of our deep human instinct and desire to find pleasure in nature.

Beyond its pleasures, however, the Calder also has its dangers, and Garrat's Linn, as well as being a place of happiness, is also known to have been a scene of tragedy. Over the centuries numerous accidental drownings have been recorded in the glen, and one particularly poignant story, from 1842, tells of a six-year-old boy, Sandy Blackburn, who went 'stravaigit with a companion up to Garrat's Linn gathering Blaeberries'. Enticed by the temptsome berries too close to the river's edge, he was said to have fallen 'head long from the craig to the linn' and drowned. His companion, unable to save him, was reportedly later found sobbing helplessly in the woods. Like much else in the wild and rugged environs of Calder Glen, Garrat's Linn evokes conflicting emotions. Its deep, dark pool, at once welcoming and threatening, resonates with memories of both joy and sorrow, of harmony and horror, of light and shadow, of life and death.

Tappilicoch

Around one kilometre north of the village of Lochwinnoch, at a point where the channel of the Calder narrows to a gorge with near vertical walls, hidden amongst the trees, obscured and almost entirely forgotten, stands a peculiar feature on the landscape: a seven-metre (or twenty-three-foot) tall rock pillar, standing perpendicular to the ground. Just what created this unusual rock formation is not entirely obvious. It appears, however, to be a singular portion of bedrock which has, to a much greater extent than the ground immediately surrounding it, withstood erosional forces. Perhaps it was formed by small changes, over many thousands of years, in the course of the river at this point: the present and previous courses combining to erode the surrounding rock on all sides, leaving this single, towering island of stone.

Though largely unknown and unnoticed today, records reveal that this unusual rock pillar was a noted curiosity in the nineteenth century, and during the tourist frenzy of the 1880s and 1890s, for those visitors who ventured so far upstream, it would have been a primary attraction. Going back much further in time, meanwhile, for the countless generations of people who lived in the vicinity of Calder Glen, and lived lives far more rooted in the landscape than we do today, it would undoubtedly have been a highly significant feature, both in the landscape and in their imaginations.

Unfortunately any knowledge of the old traditions and superstitions that our ancestors once attached to this rock pillar are long forgotten. One fragment of evidence relating to how earlier people conceptualised the stone which does survive, however, is a record of its traditional name, a name which dates from at least the eighteenth century and is perhaps much older: *Tappilicoch*.

An unusual-sounding name, Tappilicoch appears to have a hybrid Scots and Gaelic etymology: from the Scots, *Tap o' Licoch* or 'Top of Licoch', where 'Licoch' likely derives from the Gaelic *Leacach*, meaning 'flat surface', and seemingly refers to a distinctive wide and shallow section of the River Calder which is found immediately downstream from the rock pillar. To ease pronunciation, in the eighteenth and nineteenth centuries Tappilicoch was commonly shortened by locals to *Tapilico* or *Tapaleco*, with emphasis presumably resting on the first and third syllables.

Today, Tappilicoch sits in a bend of the river which is seldom visited: deep and inaccessible. It was not always so, however. Indeed records indicate that as late as the 1860s a footbridge spanned the river at this point. Evidence also suggests that in the eighteenth century there may have been habitations close to this spot on both sides of the river: on the north a cottar's house, which also seemingly acquired the name Tappilicoch, and on the south the pre-improvement farmstead of *Laigh Linthills*, which, unlike the modern farm of the same name, was said to have lain 'on the Water of Calder above the Mount Lowps'.

It is also notable that the little-documented, but once regionally significant, *Cloak* or *Shyne Castle* also stood less than two hundred metres from the site of Tappilicoch. It is perhaps not fanciful to imagine, therefore, that, from ancient times, the gorge of Tappilicoch would have been an important crossing point of the Calder. Then, as now, Tappilicoch has stood as a silent witness to the procession of humanity and remains an enduring symbol of the deep mysteries and untold stories of the glen.

Knockan Linn

Around three hundred metres upstream from Tappilicoch is the largest and undoubtedly the most spectacular of Calder Glen's waterfalls: *Knockan Linn*. A plunge waterfall where the stream drops vertically, detaching itself, momentarily, from the river bed, Knockan Linn was famed in the nineteenth century for being somewhere that visitors 'may venture to pass under the bed of the river without [getting] wet'. And while it would be easy to assume that the name Knockan Linn derives from a Gaelic origin (*knockan*

in Gaelic meaning 'a small hill'), it is perhaps just as likely to
have a Scots etymology: *knockan* or *knockin* meaning beating or
pounding, and perhaps referencing the action of the river as it
crashes down, over the rock ledge, and into its plunge pool.

Spectacular in its beauty, in the tourist boom of the late nineteenth century Knockan Linn would undoubtedly have been
one of the primary attractions of Calder Glen. Viewed from the
downstream side, the waterfall and its environs make for a captivating space: the large splash zone of the falls, creating a wide
viewing area which seems almost peculiarly adapted for human
appreciation.

The sense of wonder which such a scene evokes is easily felt, but
not so easily explained. For the religious, the experience might be
likened to witnessing something of the hand of God. For the secular,
however, it might be easier to imagine that the scene simply speaks
to something primitive in us: the fast-flowing water; the shelter of
the surrounding crags; the abundance of vegetation and wildflowers,
all suggestive of somewhere that is, at a deep and a fundamental
level, conducive to our human survival. Perhaps, though, there is
also something more complex at play: something deeper that is
stirred in our psyches by the interplay of not only the beautiful, or
harmonious features of nature, but also, what nineteenth-century
writers termed, the *sublime*, or the more fearful aspects of the wild.

At Knockan Linn one feature which certainly lends itself to the
sense of *sublime* is the dark and foreboding cave behind the falls.
Created over thousands of years by the erosional forces of the river,
this dark void, which opens into a wider chamber behind, evokes
a discomforting sense of the unknown. It is a sense which is vividly
captured in one clearly apocryphal, local myth, first recorded by
local antiquarian Andrew Crawfurd in 1840, of a piper who entered
a cave in Calder Glen (perhaps, though not certainly, this one) to
explore its dark recesses. Taking his bagpipes with him to direct
those above ground as to his movements, it is said that he was

heard 'very distinctly until he reached the Hill of Stake, about five miles distant', where, grimly, 'all traces of the piper and his musical instrument were lost'.

Another tradition relating to the cave at Knockan Linn, which is far more factual yet perhaps hints at equally deep mysteries, are accounts which state that it was here that, in the eighteenth century, two ancient quern stones were discovered by a local farmer. These quern stones, a primitive technology used for the grinding of grain, are thought to have been millennia old. Where they came from and why they were deposited in the cave is unclear. Were they simply discarded here incidentally? Or was Knockan Linn a place where at least some of our ancient ancestors chose to come and perform the seasonal, perhaps highly ritualised, task of grain grinding? If so, just what exactly it was which drew them to this site was perhaps just as much of a mystery to them then as it remains to us today.

Grizzie Montgomerie

Grizzie Montgomerie went daft about the salvation of her soul. She daunerit in her daft fits, with wee Tammie in her cleuk, about Calderbank and remote places. But she recovered before her death.

This snippet of information, recorded in 1837 by Crawfurd in his *Cairn of Lochwinnoch Matters*, describes a woman, who, if other information is to be believed, was around forty years old and living in the Old Town of Lochwinnoch, when, around the year 1750, she resorted to the glen with her child, 'wee Tammie', wrapped in her cloak, and may be the earliest surviving record of someone utilising Calder Glen as a spiritual resource.

How Crawfurd came to know of this story is not entirely clear: the events took place thirty years before he was born so it certainly wasn't first-hand knowledge. It is likely, however, that the story was passed down through the generations of Grizzie's family, and perhaps made its way to Crawfurd from Tammie himself: the infant in the story, who was, in his adult life, a near neighbour of Crawfurd's.

Though the story was recorded by Crawfurd without commentary, the reason for its inclusion in his book, and for its continued transmission over the generations, was likely the perceived strangeness of Grizzie's behaviour. The image of a young mother of unsettled mind, carrying her baby into remote and perhaps dangerous places, was, to both storytellers and audiences of the eighteenth and nineteenth centuries, likely a disturbing one. It's possible, however, to interpret the story in other ways, and from a modern perspective it is perhaps tempting to picture Grizzie as someone experiencing a form of mental distress (perhaps even post-natal depression), and her wanderings in the glen as a strategy of, what may today may be termed, 'self-help'.

From *The Cairn* we can glean some additional details of Grizzie's life which appear to add to this picture. Firstly, we learn that, having been raised at Meikle Cloak, on the very doorstep of Calder Glen, when Grizzie resorted to the glen in her adult life, she was likely returning to childhood haunts: places of long-standing, and, it may be imagined, deep, personal significance to her. Secondly, we also learn that, at the time of her wanderings, Grizzie was suffering from the recent loss of a child: her son Tammie, we learn, was one of twins, the other had 'died young'. And one final detail which adds even greater poignancy to the story, is that, Grizzie, we learn, was not her husband's first wife. The first, a Janet Tarbet, had died some years earlier in childbirth, along with the child.

The image, therefore, of Grizzie and Tammie wandering the glen, with its high crags and plunging waterfalls, can be seen as one which is highly symbolic and deeply evocative of the precariousness of life which mothers and infants have faced through so much of human history: they walked, physically and figuratively, the razor's edge. Grizzie's story can also, however, be seen as a powerful testament of human strength and resilience: the ability for women, and men, to find in places like Calder Glen meaning and beauty in their lives. From Crawfurd's concluding sentence we learn that Grizzie 'recovered before her death'. With the help of Calder Glen it appears that Grizzie was successful in surmounting her challenges.

The Lost Words

Immediately upstream from Knockan Linn can be found a sequence of waterfalls, gorges, rapids and potholes, of spectacular beauty whose traditional names appear to have been forgotten: lost to time. Now nameless, this section of river feels denuded of something of its essential character. The common names we have for features on our landscape, beyond their utility in assisting communication, also appear to help us, in a deeper way, to anchor ourselves on the landscape. Perhaps stemming from a primitive and ancient part of our psyche, where orienteering was once essential to our survival, the waterfalls of the Calder feel like important landmarks: characters on the landscape, that are deserving, and even demanding of a name.

That the waterfalls in this section of the Calder certainly, at one time, would have had traditional names seems clear. In the mid-nineteenth century, Crawfurd compiled lists of hundreds of Lochwinnoch placenames which were known to him but which have, in the years subsequent, fallen out of use. Unfortunately for us, when Crawfurd compiled his lists his interest appears to have been primarily etymological rather than topographical, and he did not record the precise locations of the placenames he enumerated. As a consequence we are left today with a plethora of placenames without a place.

For Calder Glen we learn, tantalisingly, of waterfalls and pools with names such as *Linnhead Linn, Efforsbrae Linn, Braid Linn, Sclatiefuird Linn* and *Burto's Linn*. There are also the names of tributaries such as *Snypes Burn* and *Draiglan Burn*, as well as more enigmatic and mysterious placenames such as *Gulie Aker, Widow's Fauld, Stinkan Weeds, Whytefauld Spout, Stane o' the brae* and *Tour O' Muntock*: the precise whereabouts of all of which are today unknown.

For the small number of traditional Calder placenames which we can still positively identify – names of the glen, such as Ravenscraig, Tappilicoch and Knockan Linn – it may be recognised that we have the work, chiefly, of the early Ordnance Survey to thank. In the 1860s, this newly founded national mapping agency began their first surveys of the area, and when it came to charting Calder Glen, it is clear that these early surveyors used Crawfurd's work, and in particular his 1829 descriptive records of the glen, as a guide. Using his accounts of the places described, and with the assistance of locals, they were able to nail down onto their maps, and into an enduring public record, the names of some of the glen's most conspicuous features. Even at that time, however, less than a decade after Crawfurd's death, it appears that even this was achieved with some difficulty: the surveyors writing in their reference books, of Reikan Linn, 'the name is only known among some of the old people connected with the neighbourhood'; and of Knockan Linn, 'not generally known but to those brought up in the neighbourhood'. And for the vast majority of Crawfurd's placenames, which the surveyors overlooked, it appears that a final opportunity for documentation may have been missed.

In short time after their work, and Crawfurd's death, it appears that many of these placenames fell out of memory. Words which had been passed down orally for centuries dying in the mouths of a passing generation. And so it is that the names of the beautiful waterfalls, gorges and rapids north of Knockan Linn remain lost. Which, if any, of Crawfurd's unattributed placenames belong to them can only be guessed at. There is hope, however, that with further research this may yet change. Perhaps new information will yet come to light which will allow for more of Crawfurd's lost words, currently left floating across the landscape, to find their way home. In so doing, it may be believed that we too may also, in some measure, better find our way.

Reikan Linn

Upstream from the Lost Words Cascades the banks of Calder Glen shallow considerably, the woodland fringe narrows, and for the space of around a kilometre the illusion of the glen as a 'different world' is broken, as the surrounding farm and muirland extend in places even to touch the river's edge. In the vicinity of Tandlemuir, however, around three kilometres north of Lochwinnoch, the ravine steepens once more, the woods thicken, and the glen resumes much of its previous character. And at the heart of this deep and captivating section of the glen sits yet another sublime waterfall: *Reikan Linn*.

Reikan Linn appears to have a Scots etymology: *reikan*, translating to English as 'smoking', and presumably referencing the spray and mists that form around the base of these falls when the river is in spate. Other than its name, however, no other specific traditions surrounding this waterfall survive. Difficult to access and at a considerable distance to the village, Reikan Linn is seldom visited today, and for the same reasons has likely attracted relatively few visitors for many centuries past. What stories this place may once have held appear to have been forgotten: washed away in the unceasing current of time.

In imagining how our more distant ancestors may have interpreted such an enigmatic feature on the landscape as Reikan Linn, it is perhaps instructive to remember that as little as three centuries ago a belief in the presence of supernatural powers was widespread. For our early modern ancestors, magic was as real as the ground under their feet and a fundamental part of how people rationalised and explained the world around them. And that Calder Glen was seen, in particular, as a 'place of magic' – somewhere that strange things could and did happen – is evidenced in numerous fragments of local folklore preserved by Andrew Crawfurd in the early nineteenth century.

Amongst a wide range of beliefs recorded by Crawfurd, on the hopeful side it was thought that the waters of individual waterfalls could contain certain healing qualities: for example, *Sorrow Linn*, on the Cloak burn at the foot of the glen, was reputedly 'famous for the cure of madness'. While benevolent brownies (elf-like creatures) were also thought to have lived in the glen, such as those who were thought to have charitably set Robert Kirkwood's *New Mill of Calder* into operation one night. More sinisterly, however, the glen was also somewhere that you might expect to encounter malevolent spirits: spirits such as the witch who one Elizabeth Jamieson was said to have encountered when traversing the glen one evening in the early eighteenth century. And reputed to live in the deep pools of the rivers around Lochwinnoch were also the fearsome kelpies: shape-shifting water spirits who dragged unsuspecting individuals to their deaths.

From today's perspective these folkloric beliefs can appear highly peculiar, almost bizarre, and perhaps threaten to alienate us from our ancestors and their way of thinking. When considered more fully, however, these stories also have the potential to do the opposite. In revealing something of our ancestors' anxieties and insecurities these tales can offer an insight into a way of thinking which is perhaps not so dissimilar to our own as we may think. From a functionalist analysis these beliefs would certainly not have persisted if they did not serve a purpose. And considering the mythology of the kelpies in particular it is easy to see a very practical benefit to this mythology in warning people, especially young children, away from dangerous stretches of water. Whether kelpies lived in the deep, dark waters of Reikan Linn or not, as our ancestors came to learn through painful experience, it was perhaps best to behave like they did.

Ellis Jamieson
STOLON

We find the cat.

Through the forest, we follow the sound of trapped fluttering from sun-bleached *Missing* posters nailed to trees and, eventually, the taste of those *Missing* posters after they come loose and turn to mulch inside the earth. Pecked free by birds who didn't like their wind-wrought thrashing, they come apart – dissolve – until their threads resemble ours. But the nails remain embedded in the tree. The birds couldn't remove them.

We follow the ragged breathing of the crows and soft pad of foxes' feet. We follow the hum of the flies and the whisper of ants among the fallen leaves and the drone of hungry wasps that hunt them to eat.

We find her under a branch, bare of leaves and sharp from where the wind has ripped it from its socket. Not a big branch, but big enough and strong enough to fasten her to the earth with one long spike. We taste the wood first, old rain and rot held just inside the bark. Our mycelium quivers at the taste.

We find her from below. The dark, metallic soil, swollen and heavy with the parts of her that drained, makes us lingeringly rich and full. We spread and grow in feathered fingers through the peaty soil, coiling up to cradle her with limbs of bloodless veins. She waits for us, pinned like all those *Missing* posters to the earth by one sharp point.

Her body has long since stopped moving for the second time, fur no longer rippling as flies' nests tend to make it do. Deflated mats of bark-brown fur cling to what their offspring could not eat. We find her bones inside like ruined monuments. Our fingers brush them. Hold them. Sink inside their marrow, and wonder that they moved so freely, without root, and leaving naught but pawprints in their wake.

We hold her. We remember the beat of silent padding as she hunted birds and mice for us to eat. We remember the pin-prick cut of claws in our rotten bark when she fled up our trees to hide from off-lead dogs. We remember transitory warmth and tasting cast-off fur from cosy summer days spent on the forest floor together. The waste she left. The vibrations of her purr. The there-and-goneness of her.

Her empty sockets are like open doors. Her teeth, the only remnants not abstract and still definitively feline. We mould ourselves to her shape and spread between the gaps in her as if we'd pull her back together.

Through the open doors we watch: stars and suns and clouds and moons. Rain comes and goes and comes again. The crows caw loudly, but they won't touch her anymore. No more beaks to pick the tender bits of her, or claws to carry them away. She's too clean for them. Once, one flies down to peck the silver, mud-stained disk that marks her throat, and we remember how it used to jingle – soft, like water singing. The crow sees us watching him; black sockets full of black eyes full of us. Silent, he flaps his hurried wings and flies away. Crows are clever birds.

Eventually, we're full enough. We bloom inside her, pushing up the wisps of mud-bound fur and reaching out into the air. More and more and more of us we make, with caps of creamy mourning white to commemorate. Celebrate. Rejuvenate. Breaking down and building up, sharing her with the forest. Our forest.

*

They find us in the passing of another storm. We hear them through the roots, and in the frantic flight of birds. We hear them in the rush of rabbits skittering into burrows, and in the silence that always follows human feet.

By small, brown boots we're found. The soil trembles in their tread. A scream. A wail. They're gone again. Soon more boots come and, far above, the eyes of those we'll never eat gaze down. We feel the rain in them. They *pit pat pit* on our sticky caps and we wonder if this is how they taste. Of salt. Of angry pain and sorrow.

The boot comes down. It breaks our necks and splits our heads. Again, again we're kicked and scraped from our poor cat and dashed to dirt, pink gills exposed and bleeding spores.

The limbs of us inside the earth are next. We feel the teasing, tearing of her bones being pulled – uprooted from the earth. We cling to her – our cat. Our fingers bleed and tear and snap. We lose her to the air. They carry her away. One, like distant thunder rumbles,

We'll give her a proper burial.

Underneath the weight of her cortege, twigs and brown, dead leaves crunch and crack. We have no eyes to see her go, but feel it like exposed nerves in teeth. Cold wind tumbles over us. Our mycelium forest shivers. We lick the wound of her. Crows fly between the thick, grey clouds, and the insects of the forest investigate the absence of her bones. Slowly, cautious, quiet; leaning down upon the roots of living trees, we feel our way back inside the earth.

Then, somewhere far, yet not so far away that parts of us aren't already there, the earth is disturbed below a lonely, isolated tree. Our cat's familiar bones are placed inside in shrouds of ancient towels, and covered up and stamped firmly down to keep the grassy earth above pristine. The soil's wound will heal in time. We shall knit it back together with the rain.

Like autumn days, rain comes, rain goes. We reach. We curl inside her. We find her and, piece by peaceful piece, we bring her home again.

Ioulia Kolovou

[A BILINGUAL DICTIONARY OF LOSS &
MOURNING WEAVED WITH FRAGMENTS
FROM A JOURNAL]

Extracts A to E

[Prologue – Fragment 241019]
One month, two weeks, and three days have passed since that
cold grey evening, grey September, grey streets, grey motorways –
M8 'the friendly motorway' not so friendly-looking just a few
metres away from the entrance of the Royal – grey buses, under-
passes, people rushing home after the last final shop of the day
to tea and to TV. And inside, bright lights, too bright but not
inside the ICU, where I see you, for one last time I see you. On
your deathbed. I sit at your deathbedside. Deathbedside manner.
Manner of speaking.

It still surprises me how much we people, we poor people, we
poor wee people, whippoorwills, how we fear death and its apparatus and its very name.

D.E.A.T.H.

Don't. Even. Ask. Too. Hot.

Scalding. Singeing. Scorching.

During the terrible years and months and weeks and days before,
while R. was alive and he suffered and we suffered I often wished
for death to come, for him, for me, for the whole world. In my head
I composed funeral orations. His. Mine. The world's. A strange
consolation. Like putting a full stop at the very last sentence of a
book. Like writing The End after days and weeks and months
and years of hard labour. Prison. We were all prisoners then. When
R. was alive and alcoholic and abusive and we suffered I fled the
flat and I walked in the streets and everything looked as if it was
made of iron, heavy, oppressive, unyielding. I put one foot ahead
of the other, trudging on, this is it, this is how it feels to be in a
hard labour camp, this heavy treading under unimaginable pressure.

Composing his funeral oration is my head was a source of some comfort and relief. But now that he is dead –

I think of death and it is scary and sad, like when a terrified wife's trying to appease an alcoholic husband. A terrified child trying to appease a violent father. Someone who was not always like that. Someone we loved and lost and found and lost.

Anakomidē

(n.) A harvest of bones.

Three years after the burial, the bones of the dead are dug up in the presence of close family – those who can bear it – and a priest. They are washed in wine and water, wrapped up lovingly in a white linen cloth, chanted over, blessed. ('How can this small thing be his fine head?' my mother wondered, holding my father's skull, unknowingly evoking Shakespeare.) Then they are placed in the ossuary, in the company of all the other bones of ancestors, of friends who went before them, of fellow citizens, of strangers. They will stay in that company for eternity. Until a voice calls them to rise, and flesh and skin and hair grows back on them, ready for life eternal. Or, in another version of the future, until they are ground to dust and absorbed back into the elements, in the centuries and in the millennia to come, which is as good as eternity, I guess, for us humans, *whose days are short as grass, as flowers in the field.*

[Fragment 010919]

R. is in hospital, dying, apparently. I saw my sister-in-law's message at 1:30 a.m.; I was going to bed later than usual. I called her back just before 2 a.m. and we spoke for an hour. She's staying at the Premier Inn in the city centre, near City Chambers.

Here's the gist of it:

He was taken to hospital last Saturday and has been in there for a week, between the high dependency unit and the ICU. So far, the diagnosis is respiratory pneumonia and encephalitis. Kidneys and liver have given up. But his heart is strong, and he may yet live, although his quality of life will be very low, vegetative, more or less. They are not expecting him to recover this time; yet he may. I'm thinking of R. in a hospital bed down the road, unconscious and twitching in his encephalitis-induced sleep, the colour of mahogany, fighting for – or against – his life.

I have been expecting this phone call. Now that it's come, it feels more like fiction than reality, a script someone wrote for some people who are not we.

Bury
(v.) To tuck the dead in bed.
Antigone, the eponymous character in the Greek play written and performed for the first time in 441 BCE, dies because she refuses to leave the body of her brother unburied. Declared an enemy of the state, he has been left to rot out in the fields, *a tasty treasure for dogs and vultures to find*. But Antigone defies the explicit orders and buries her brother in secret. The first time, undetected. Everyone believes it's a rebel group defying the King. The second, when she returns to complete the rites, she is caught.

How did she manage to bury him, twice, no group of hardened rebels but a girl alone against the law? She covered his body in handfuls of thin dust, she poured libations three, wine and milk and water, she wailed bitterly and tore her hair and clothes. With those acts, she performed the prescribed ancient rites, she *rendered to Those Below what was theirs*. For those acts, she died.

The verb for bury in the ancient text is *kryptein* = to hide under the earth. That's where the word crypt comes from. A hiding place for the dead.

Elephants also bury their dead, covering them in dust.

[Fragment 020919]
I stay with R. for about an hour.

It is a strange, unreal experience to be with him in the same room and see him again after eight months. The last time we were in a room alone, he tried to strangle me, dishevelled and delirious, wild strangers lurking behind his eyes. This time the sight is not scary, not upsetting, quite the opposite, good after years of pure badness. I suppose this has something to do with the fact that he had been alcohol-free for nearly two weeks now. His skin clear from ulcers, his hands and feet soft, his fingernails long but white, not a trace of black, his beard and hair cut short and washed.

They care well for him in hospital. *The unclean spirits went out.* But the mark of death is upon him: his skin is thick, waxy, a deep tawny yellow, like jaundice – his liver is completely cirrhotic now. He looks a little like a prophet, all high forehead and deep-set eyes and aquiline nose and sharp cheekbones, venerable in spite of the tubes and drip feeds sticking out of his head and hands and body like tendrils.

He is peaceful, that's why he looks good to my eyes, if pitiful in his total weakness and dependence on the machines (eighty per cent of his oxygen comes from the machine). Gone is the wild and evil look; the *legion* that had taken possession and peeped out of his eyes have gone; he is beyond their reach now.

Charon

(n.) Proper name, pronounced Khāron. Also Charos, or Charontas. A personification of Death. In European folklore he's the Grim Reaper, a skeleton with an enormous scythe. In Ancient Greek mythology, Charon is the ferryman who takes the dead over the Lake Acherousia, the Black, Joyless Lake, to Hades, on a journey of no return. Coins were placed on the eyes of the dead for their fare. There is a funny story by Lucian of Samosata about a dead penniless philosopher who tried to trick Charon into returning him to the world of the living, since he did not have the fare to travel further into the world of the dead.

In the centuries after Antiquity, in Greek folk songs, Charon, who is now known as Charos or Charontas, is a splendidly dressed rider on a gigantic black horse in gold and silver harness. He has a wife, Charontissa, and children, the Charontakia. The Charon family house is filled with all the wealth in the world, which inevitably ends up there. Charon is merciless: he snatches people, babies off their mothers' arms, young brides off the altar, strong young men, the old and the sick. He makes no distinctions of age, rank, wealth: a true egalitarian. He takes the dead, indifferent to their pleas and cries, on a miserable ride to the Underworld, where he makes them servants and slaves in his household. Sometimes they try to argue with him, but he is not as naïve as Lucian's story makes him out to be. *The World Below is the place from where no one returns.*

In a Medieval Greek epic, a hero called Digenes Akritas, the strongest man of his era, fought Charon in single combat on a threshing floor made of marble. The fight went on for three days and nights. After a valiant fight, Digenes was thrashed on the marble floor.

[Fragment 030919]

I dream of people *who are dead or lost to me as if they were dead.* I had to walk through the sea to reach them. A cluster of sea urchins just under the surface of the water, black and spiky and perfectly round; I picked my way carefully through them, stepping on the slippery stones.

No news from the hospital. The last update, last night at around 9 p.m., was that his temperature was up a little. When I tell Mama, she says that this is a very bad sign. Bad for whom? I know what Mama thinks: it's the best for everyone, including R. himself, that he dies. It will just be formalising something that has been happening for a long time now. The man we knew and loved died years ago. But what does that even mean? He's still living, and he may yet come out of the hospital alive. It won't be the first time that someone who's been written off is snatched back *from Charon's teeth.* Only, is that R. or the usurper who lived in his place these last several years?

Let me not beautify the past because R. is ill in hospital, possibly dying. He was good and loveable once. He had all the best intentions in the world. He loved me and A., he really did. But love could not conquer his self-destructive compulsion. The loving, caring, sensitive, funny, talented man was gradually replaced by the cruel, demented, selfish, soulless spawn of chemical dependency and addiction.

I tried to explain to A. what was happening to his dad using the plot of the Invasion of the Body Snatchers. He seemed to get it, and I'm sure he'll look the film up. He's interested in all sorts of pop culture lately, and he knows much more than I know. I hope it helps him to make sense of it all. Because I can't really.

On the way to his guitar lesson in the East End, we passed the Royal, and again on the return home. It was dusk by then, and I showed him where his dad was, just a few metres away from us, in an ICU bed. I made up another story about our imaginary pets, the dog Brasidas and the cat Aristeides, who bear the names of the Spartan and Athenian rivals from one of the great wars in Antiquity and speak in human voices and are involved in all sorts of comical situations. I first began to make up those stories for him when we walked to his school in the morning, having tiptoed out of the flat like cat burglars to avoid waking up R. and setting off the madness. Then I would tell him another story at bedtime in his room, where we both slept with a chair jammed against the door to keep us safe during the night. Our imaginary pets kept us safe and sane throughout the terrible last two year of R.'s vertiginous descend into Hades. We laughed our way through that horror. In these stories, the world became a light-hearted, sunny, kindly place, where we could laugh and find relief from the netherworld into which R. was plunging and pulling us along.

Laughter saved us; we still laugh. To see the funny side of even the darkest situation is a gift. It's one of the things they always said about A. at school: how much he enjoys jokes, puns, and banter; how they love to see his smile light up his face.

I hope we laugh for a very long time still; I hope we always find things to laugh about. I hope that the sense of fun and of the ridiculousness of most things, which softens the heart and makes forgiveness so much easier, never leaves us.

Dream Visions

Two days before he died, my father had a dream vision. He saw that an angel of the Lord came to him holding a scroll, like the ones holy figures are holding in Greek Orthodox icons. The angel showed him the scroll and tore it up and said: This is the contract of your debt. It is now forgiven. You are free.

My father took this to mean that he was absolved from his bondage to addiction. A smoker and drinker throughout his life from his early teens until nearly the end, even though he suffered from debilitating heart disease, he decided that he should die a free man. So he went into hospital – my mother and his doctors were begging him to do this for a long time but he had refused – because that was the only place where he would not be able to drink or smoke.

He was in for two days. The third day, he suffered cardiac arrest. When the doctors rushed in to resuscitate him, he made a signal to them not to. He said: 'Can't you see he's already here? Saint George is here to escort me out.' He was smiling and his face was bright and happy when he died.

'Your father was – extraordinary,' the doctor told my other sister, who wasn't present at the moment of his departure, later. 'I've never witnessed anything like that before.'

Dream visions and other visions that we would probably call hallucinations or vivid dreams now were nothing extraordinary for people who lived (or still live) in what we call the pre-modern era. Those visions were from heaven – or from hell. Patristic texts mention dream visions of temptation by demons. Contrary to the common prurient belief, those were not mainly sexual (even though the most famous are, which says more about the audience than the storytellers), but nightmares of sadness and despair. Most people who report dream visions in the country of my birth usually see angels, or saints, or the Virgin Mary. The faithful are protected in sleep. But for most of us, dreams are the rendezvous point where we meet the dead we loved and lost.

[Fragment 050919]
On this day, at ten minutes to seven, R. died, peacefully, free from bondage to alcohol, reconciled with the people who loved him best, clean and fresh and innocent like a baby. I was sitting next to him, holding his hand throughout, and his sister was sitting there too, and the hum of the cricket on the radio – he never missed it when alive – and it was sweet and bitter to see him go quietly, like a lamb, and all was forgiven.

No reproach or bitterness left.

Good night, R. Goodbye. I only weep because this is goodbye forever, because there is no place in this world where I can ever find you again.

Dust
(n.) The earth, ground in fine grains.
We all end up dead, *dust upon dust*; the earth is straining under the weight of so many dead people; the ground is made of bones ground in the great mill of time. No one remembers most of the people whose remaining particles make up the earth on which we step and which will eventually hide us. And if some are remembered, what does it matter to them now?

Eis Hadou Kathodos
(tr.) Descent into Hades, Journey into the Underworld.
Inanna. Orpheus, Herakles, Theseus. Odysseus. God, demigods, heroes made that journey to the place *whence nobody returns*. They all went willingly, albeit not happily, looking for someone, or something. A person, a dog, information. They all came back,

some successful in their quest, some unsuccessful. Some barely escaped with the help of a divine adviser, others had to provide an exchange, someone who would be taken back there in their place.

In the Christian tradition, there is a time between Crucifixion and Resurrection when Christ is dead. But this death, exactly like all the dead in Greek folk tradition, is not nonexistence. It is a journey to the Underworld. Greek Orthodox iconography does not depict the Resurrection, as opposed to the Western tradition, in which Christ pops up from a tomb, like Jack-in-the-Box, amidst discarded tombstones and tumbled soldiers. Instead, the only icon that truly traditional Greek churches will display at Easter is known by the descriptive title Eis Hadou Kathodos (interpretatively translated into English as The Harrowing of Hell), in which the focus is on the epic journey and what happens there. Christ, dressed all in white inside a glory (= an almond-shaped pod) of star-studded, brilliant light, is descending into a dark, rocky, cavernous realm. On his right and left are groups of huddled people, crowned kings, bearded philosophers and prophets, common men and women, all looking scared and startled, as if awoken from a deep sleep to face a wondrous and terrifying sight. Christ extends his arms and grabs the hand of a very old man – Adam – to his right and a very old woman – Eve – to his left, pulling them upwards. The crowds are hanging on to Adam and Eve's robes, and they are all pulled up towards the light. Beneath Christ's feet are the broken gates of the Underworld, an assortment of keys and locks lying useless on the ground. A wild-haired, bearded man, Hades himself, is sitting nearby. His dejected posture, elbow on knee, hand cupping his chin, is the semiotic representation of suffering or distress in Byzantine iconography. That, and the mournful, resigned expression on his face signify acceptance of his defeat.

And yet, traditional laments from all over Greece, from *The Iliad* and *The Odyssey* to demotic songs, still speak of *the place whence nobody returns*, totally unconvinced about that victory.

Ruby Lawrence
MOULTING

A girl contorts her spine into a back bend. Repeating this movement along the shoreline, she loops herself into tight O-shapes, watched by drunk parents. I wince as her vertebrae compress to form each strained arch. Her ribs pop out and I think of a lobster trap. My toes flick impatiently in the sand, skin glistening with shards of long-dead molluscs. The ocean does not appear to be calming down.

I remember being in Waterstones with a friend last month and we saw a book about beachcombing, or wild swimming, by a fellow white woman, and we jointly pondered just how many semi-autobiographical books about beachcombing or wild swimming the industry can sell to other white women before supply and demand become unsustainably imbalanced, one way or the other.

I despise beachcombing. I despise beaches. The ocean is boring. I like lying. I am a better liar than I am a swimmer, and I'm not a bad swimmer. I can do butterfly for one length.

My thoughts are rehearsing themselves as writing, which is disgusting, but what can I do about it? I commit to de-romanticising everything, which is difficult. My next stylised thought was going to be *it had been a year of endings*. Jesus Christ. *It had been a year of endings.*

Ugh, fuck it, by this point the horse has bolted, so go on then – the ocean is a she, divine salty feminine, yes, she's absolutely raging today, and I need her help in scouring me clean in a rough fashion so all those 'endings' can be symbolically and somatically washed away. To be a woman is to be observed observing your own writing as it wades into the gendered foam.

Tender, frayed, leftover bits. That's what I want washed away, I think. Feelings that should have departed by now. Lobsters shed their exoskeleton in one strenuous process again and again throughout their lives, and apparently it is exhausting for them.

Shut up. There is only so much you can keep at it with the lobster, loading it up with all this affective and comparative labour. Stop excavating the lobster.

Squealing kids are being plucked and dumped into the breakers by her, the ocean. Then they are blasted with sand, before crawling out onto dry land. The shoreline is littered with these shiny little squibs, panting and giggling with the outrageousness of it all. I wade past them, keeping my distance.

I manage to swim under the most aggressive, white-capped waves, pushing out beyond them. I am impressed by myself, but then a lifeguard whistles and gestures at me to come back in and I feel slightly embarrassed.

Getting back in is a problem. Consider this: *you cannot bargain with the ocean.* I accidentally swallow some water and gag. I do a tiny wee. You can't though, can you? You cannot get only what you want out of the interaction. Not like when people you haven't met yet try to arrange to come over to your flat and shag you, through a dating app. They are not interested in being friends, they are only interested in sex. But you've never smelt them. Imagine not being into someone's smell, but the interaction is decided, fate is sealed, and you've got to go through with it. *Just say no,* I've been advised. But it is easier for me to lie than to say no. To say no. To speak that word and intend it, to trust it, to trust it, to act upon the world. Well, well, well. Isn't that a nice idea. My lower lip has been bitten open by one of my teeth and the blood tastes pathetic. This whole thing is starting to feel less amusing.

I am dragged away from the shore each time I kick towards it, and I can't hear the kids anymore. A house-sized wave approaches. Slams. Certain things are decided.

*

Tonight, I will aggressively brush at black sand planted so firmly and deeply in the skin of my belly and groin that I will not be able to remove it with fingers alone. Such pressure. I do not know this yet because I'm currently tremoring under a towel after managing finally to get out, and the girl is still making O-shapes. I am now a blob. No lingering feelings. One bleeding knee.

I watch three swimmers enter the heaving ocean. The lifeguards let them go. They are lean, wiry people who plough out firm and fluid in a straight line; their front crawl has a slicing confidence to it. I want to stumble after them and ask *what did you do to earn the lifeguard's trust? Do you have a pre-existing relationship? Or do the lifeguards read something in your bodies, something immediately apparent, in the way you meet the water?*

One day maybe I'll be waved past by lifeguards and have their absolute confidence, because I will be so undeniably good at swimming.

I warm up in the heat of the sun and become sleepy, drifting under a damp towel draped over my body like a burial shroud. The light is mellow in here. I suck like a kitten on the towel's label, which tastes of indoors. My fingers are squished inside the waistband of my shorts in an attempt to feel tucked in, secure.

One day maybe I, so certain, will say *no*, and shed my exoskeleton for the first time.

Some remnant sea-taste creeps up my throat so I languidly turn my head to one side, letting the label fall from my mouth. I spit onto the face of the beach, then return to stillness.

This future shedding of mine, the first of many, will hurt for sure, but my *no* will be loud and affirmative. Matter will lie afterwards crumpled on the sand like an old jacket, and I will be inscrutable and contrary. I will eat some of the matter, macerating it with my sharp teeth. And I will tell some more lies, and my new shell will be brilliant blue and red and I will lie some more, and my *no* will be so loud and clear, fierce as sunlight, and I will be suspicious, on the day I say *no*, I will be suspicious. If to be a woman is to be observed then which one to watch, in that fleeting moment of shedding? The still-warm, peeling jacket, or the emergent body? The quiet mouth, nibbling on its own *no*?

Hannah Ledlie
SLEEPER

woken by the false chorus of 4 a.m. –
birds calling for company
then falling back to sleep –
I unzip the balcony and watch
a naked freight train streak
through the darkness

THE EMBROIDERY

My grandma got as far as a butterfly,
two bluebells and a daisy,
then I guess she got bored
or ran out of thread.

Decades later my mother finished
the rest. A panorama
of botanical inaccuracies:
species belonging to separate seasons,
separate soils, planted
on one beige canvas.

I think we all need two funerals:
first the public unravelling,
then a quiet project we stitch
together in the evenings.

Kate McAllan
GERRY

I was doing my makeup in the back seat of the car, applying eyeshadow with my finger which fell in flakes down my face. We were on our way to my uncle's funeral and it was a day when too much was happening. My parents sat in the front seats, my mum staring quietly in that way which makes you wonder what she's thinking.

It was raining by now and that was a shame. For all the people standing at the graveside, but also because I had plans later on. We stood at the space in the cemetery listening to the minister make jokes about my uncle. He was listing all the nicknames that people used to call him.

And who could forget his terrific sense of humour, said the minister, smiling.

I thought about the time he got drunk and pissed into the fireplace of my parent's front room. Everybody said it had been my dad's large measures, but really he had been drunk when he'd arrived that morning. It was quiet as they lowered his coffin into the ground. My aunt threw a flower into the grave as a piper began to play.

The wake was at his favourite pub in the East End, at one point he'd actually lived in the flat above. His friends gathered round shaking their heads and pouring red wine into glasses. I downed a cup of coffee and ate a sandwich really fast, cleaning my teeth with my finger. I was meeting Alexander, a boy I liked from school, and I couldn't wait to leave. A woman in a fur coat was crying and trying to talk to me, but I didn't know who she was and no one else could say either. I squeezed her on the shoulder and said some quick goodbyes and then ran out for the train to town. Now the day felt suddenly lighter, less grey.

The weather in reality was still terrible though and nothing like I'd hoped for when I'd been imagining the day. I wandered up and down Buchanan Street, dipping in to several shops and thinking about Alexander. I was thinking about all the hours we'd have together. The day was full of possibility. I sat on a bench to wait and almost like in a movie the sky began to brighten. I spotted him in the crowd. He was standing far away and it looked like he hadn't seen me though probably he had. Eventually our eyes met, his hands were buried deep in his pockets. He had an expression on his face which was impossible to read. I smiled.

I'm just back from a funeral, I told him. It was all I could think to say.

Sorry, said Alexander. Was it someone close?

My uncle. Though not through blood. He was with my aunt for years though.

Oh right, he said.

He began to walk.

And what did he die of?

Lots of different things. He didn't keep well. There was someone playing bagpipes at the graveyard and I didn't know what he'd think of that.

Why? said Alexander.

Well, he didn't like that kind of thing. He liked dance music.

Was he a war hero?

What? I said and I laughed.

No.

I thought they only played pipes for war heroes, said Alexander. He frowned.

He wasn't like that at all, I said and then I laughed a lot more but maybe I shouldn't have.

It's nice to see you, I said.

He looked embarrassed.

Oh yes, he nodded. Yes it's good to see you too.

We took a bus to be where we had to go and then we waited in line outside a tent. It was my idea that we should go to the circus.

It seemed a much better idea than the cinema or the park and I was sure it would be memorable. Something we couldn't forget.

I loved the circus when I was younger, I told Alexander.

He turned to smile at me for the first time that day.

The guy at the door punched our tickets. He was wearing a tight t-shirt and looked about our age. Inside we found our plastic fold-down chairs and waited for the show to begin. I took two small bottles of wine I had stolen from the funeral and handed one to him. He looked embarrassed again, but unscrewed the cap.

By the time the show started I had drunk most of the wine and the excitement was carrying me along. All I'd eaten was the sandwich in the morning. I was laughing. And sometimes so was Alexander. But soon the acts seemed repetitive. They seemed like variations of the same thing. It wasn't much like I'd remembered it from when I was a kid. Everything seemed loud and the cast seemed a little weary, like maybe we were the last show of the season.

A man with cages of yellow canaries came out balancing them on sticks. There were a couple of small dogs riding scooters at one point, which went on for way too long. In the end though, I felt most sorry for the elephant, especially when the trapeze artist wrapped her legs around its neck. She was wearing a pale blue leotard and her long dark hair hung down to the floor.

Do you think she's beautiful, I whispered.

Alexander shrugged.

She is, he said.

And I agreed. But as I watched her I felt a bad feeling that I sometimes get. It happens when a thought arrives and the rest of my thoughts begin to escalate. At first I was thinking of the beautiful trapeze artist. I was thinking that Alexander may never try to kiss me. Soon, I felt the disappointment of the day fall over me like a blanket. And then suddenly I was thinking of my uncle in the ground. The rain falling on the grass of the cemetery. I looked around the audience and I looked at all the faces. I told Alexander I had to go to the toilet and then I stood in the cubicle for fifteen minutes. When I got back to my seat there was manic sounding music playing and a motorbike circling the stage.

Are you enjoying it, I asked Alexander. But he couldn't hear me. I wished that it was over.

*

On our way to the train station after the show, Alexander asked if he could go to an off license to buy some beer.

I might stop off at this party, he told me.

He had a cousin who was a student at the Uni.

You can come, said Alexander and then he held out both hands to me and widened his eyes.

I told Alexander I already had plans as per the rules I had established years before. It was important never to show boys how they made you feel. I decided I could never suggest we meet again, the event had been a failure. But at least he could now go on to the party. Whatever happened there might eclipse his memory of the day. He put his hand in to his pocket again and pulled out his brother's driving licence. I began to think up a fake place I could say I was going to but in the end I didn't. And we hugged on the platform. He left.

I bought a bag of wine gums and ate them at the bus stop. The bus was forty-five minutes away and it was the long route via Motherwell, but I didn't care. There was rain falling into the river in wide sheets. The streetlights seemed blurred through the bus shelter window. An old lady stood next to me with a plastic tied round her neck. I sat back and shut my eyes and tried to think about nothing. But soon I was thinking about my uncle again. About the days when I was younger and I'd spend weekends at his house. And I thought about a moment one day in his garden. I walked across the grass not wearing any shoes. And

I stood on something which made my skin tingle. Later I knew it was a bee. It stung me and the pain ran through my body in small surges. I fell on to my knees and I cried because there wasn't much else to do. And then my uncle came over. His name was Gerry, his real name was Gerald. He picked me up and carried me over to the blanket he was lying on and he poured vinegar on to the sting.

When I opened my eyes I saw there was a new person in the bus stop. He had a backpack over his shoulder and wore glasses like Alexander.

Do you know if this bus has come yet, he asked.

I knew he was talking to me as he was looking into my eyes.

I'm waiting for it too, I told him.

He nodded. Then he unzipped the pocket of the small jacket he was wearing and began to roll a cigarette. I watched him from the corner of my eye lick the paper to seal it.

Do you live here?

Yes, I said.

But you're going to . . .?

Yeah. Just to visit family.

He looked about twenty-five, though maybe he was older.

You a student, he said. Where do you study?

At the uni, I told him. But I had a day off so I went to the circus.

The circus? He laughed.

Yeah. It wasn't that good.

He finished his cigarette. Then put his backpack on the ground. Then he sat on the thin bench beside me.

*

Later, the student with the backpack wanted to know all about my uncle. But I couldn't think about much to tell him so I told him he liked dance music. And that his name was Gerry. We were sitting at the back of the bus now and he was drinking from a flask.

You got a boyfriend?

Yes, I said.

He at the uni too, he asked.

Yes, I said then I yawned.

I won't be able to ask for your number then, he said. But this confidence kind of threw me so I gave him a pretend version anyway as he typed it in to his phone.

I'll call it so you have mine.

Oh, it's out of battery, I told him.

He nodded and we rode together at the back of the bus in silence after that. Though the student kept smiling at me so I kept smiling back. He wasn't as nice-looking as Alexander but he was older and learned that had cachet. Maybe he was studying French. Just before my stop we started kissing for ten minutes with his hands resting on the small of my back. His lips felt a little chapped and at one point he moved his tongue to the roof of my mouth which didn't feel that normal. After a while he stopped doing that though and the warmth from his hands spread up to my head and down my legs. I pulled away for one second just to look at him. Maybe it shouldn't have felt as good as that. But it did.

Donnchadh MacCàba
CÒIG MIONAIDEAN

Fuaim gheur na chiad dùdaich
a' sgoltadh tro cheò tiugh na maidne,
mar rabhadh air latha-obrach eile,
anns a' bhaile, far an do rugadh mi.

Fo chabhag na gairm 's a-mach às an doras,
a-nuas tron chlobhsa shalach is dhorcha
làn fàilidhean breun na h-oidhche,
anns a' bhaile, far an do rugadh mi.

Cruthan nan daoine crùbte, faileasach,
clachan-càsaidh cruaidh fo an casan
toit is mìrean lìn a' lìonadh nan sgamhan,
anns a' bhaile, far an do rugadh mi.

Chaidh còig mionaidean de shaorsa seachad
a' siubhal gu ceann an rathaid,
's geata a' mhuilinn air fosgladh romhpa,
anns a' bhaile, far an do rugadh mi.

Sluagh nam ban air dòrtadh a-steach,
fhad 's a bha sgreuch na dàrna dùdaich
a' cur fàilte bhagrach orra a-rithist,
anns a' bhaile, far an do rugadh mi.

Latha fada eile a' feitheamh orra
san fhactaraidh thrang 's fhuaimneach,
a' fighe is a' snìomh gun fhois no allsachd,
anns a' bhaile, far an do rugadh mi.

Hayli McClain
IN ALL ITS MOVING PARTS

Kaydy let crowd-movement and sun-glare and sudden whims guide her from one show to the next. She accepted every desperate ten-minutes-till-curtain discount ticket hocked at her by the wanna-be friends of wanna-be artists.

On the overcrowded train that morning, while teens talked sex and business commuters cursed the whole month, Kaydy's seat companion glanced her up and down, assessing. Then he said, 'Fringe?'

'Yes.' Kaydy's answer came with a dreamlike lilt; she'd been entranced with the rolling-by of the countryside, mist burning off the hills as sunlight erased the memories of yesterday's rain. Funny how scenes were changed so seamlessly.

'Half the shows are shite, anyway,' the man told her.

Kaydy shrugged. Each day that month, she'd made her pilgrimage to Edinburgh. Quality had nothing to do with it. She worshipped the ever-ongoing act of creation in the cathedral of live theatre. The clumsier the show, the easier it was to discern its sacred workings. So she frequented Shakespeare-adjacent-to-the-park performances and filled seats for absent parents at school recitals, and she loved Fringe from top to bottom.

'I saw a "show" at Fringe, once,' the man said. 'Really, it was some tosser in denial about his useless degree in socio-transbender-po-litico performance art.'

Kaydy smiled, not even listening.

*

'Show at three?'

A new hand offered a new flyer. Kaydy accepted it. Another day – one of Fringe's final – waned warmly over Edinburgh, and she could feel something – something strange and lovely – nesting inside her. She wondered if she might be close to discovering God. Maybe Jesus was a theatre-kid, after all. He'd worked carpentry. He could have built set pieces.

Kaydy went to the show at three, unsure what it was about, or what it was even called.

She sat in the aisle of the audience, very front. Small crowd. They often were, at Fringe. The stage was small, too, and there were only two actors. Two actors and two props. Kaydy gazed at the chair, wondering where they got it from. Maybe a charity shop. A *chair*ity shop. Ha. She grinned at her own silly thought, as though the freedom of absurdity was an intoxicant spoiling the oxygen to her brain more brilliantly than any happy wee drug ever could. Such was the power of the stage.

Maybe that chair relished its part as deeply as its human co-stars did.

*

Her favourite moment of Fringe had happened three nights earlier.

A play. An actor carrying a basket of apples during Act One Scene One. Pivotal, plot-inciting things occurred, probably, but Kaydy never watched theatre for the stories, only for the makings. The actor was suddenly (carefully, as choreographed) thrown to the ground, so the basket tumbled, apples scattered, but one – one of them had – rolled off the stage, over the very edge of its known universe, alchemised from honeycrisp to wax by the process.

It rolled.

It came to a rest between Kaydy's shoes in the front row.

She stared down at it for the rest of the show. It became the centre of all reality.

At the end, after curtain-call, Kaydy picked up the prop apple. A thrill brightened her blood. She held a holy relic. She delivered it to the disillusioned stage crawling with ordinary people in cheap costumes and bad makeup.

She said, 'Excuse me . . .?'

They were rushing to prepare for the next performance; Fringe ran its players ragged.

'Excuse me. Excuse me!' Kaydy tapped a performer on the shoulder. They turned, bewildered, as though Kaydy had broken through the veil of another world. She offered him the prop apple.

'This fell off the stage,' she said softly.

'Oh, cheers – thanks – and thanks for coming – hope you enjoyed the show!'

'I did.' Kaydy was fluttering on the brink of something, knowing she'd never again experience quite what she had just experienced. 'I loved it. More than I can say.'

*

The show began. Or, rather, *before* it began, there was the beginning:

In the beginning, there was darkness, with shadows moving discreetly through it. The shadows weren't actors. Not while the lights were down. They were caught between identities – neither themselves nor their roles – in affected between-scene privacy.

The actress positioned her chair stage-left.

The actor positioned his modified prop-camera stage-right.

Lights up; let there be theatre.

Kaydy studied the actor's face as his lips formed every syllable, flared every inflection. Consonants cutting clearly. Vowels well-rounded. And the actress's makeup – did she apply it herself? How would it keep or crack under the heat of production?

People sat rapt by the story. Kaydy lost herself detecting every almost-error the actors so gracefully side-stepped. Like freckles, mistakes made the face more beautiful.

The end of the show drew near.

Kaydy's ribcage felt eggshell-delicate. Something with wings was within, wanting to break free. It didn't hurt. It never frightened her. She leaned into it. She let the sensation swell to overcome her – like an epiphany, an orgasm, a prophetic vision from Heaven – and—

The actress stood spotlighted and wrung blood from her heart for a soliloquy that pierced even the thickest armour of Fringe-doubters. Her tone tore through the listening, breath-held hush.

—and Kaydy slouched forward from her seat.

Before she could crumple to the floor, she transformed: a bird, with a sweet voice that sang, sang as it darted through and over and around the soon screaming audience. The soliloquy halted, spell broken. Life is fleeting. So fleeting. That's what live theatre has over film, in capturing the human experience. Films are dead butterflies pinned perfect to a board: beautiful but inconsequential. In live theatre, you're watching the actors age before your eyes, and anything could happen – *anything*. Someone might forget their lines. Someone might have a heart attack. Someone might turn into a bird. Someone has.

The director tripped over unoccupied seats to open a door. The bird flew into the hall, where a ticket-checker dropped his phone with a startled 'Bloody h—' left unfinished. He wrenched open a humidity-swelled window that fought back.

The bird vanished into a blue sky over bustling Edinburgh.

*

Awkward laughter. Seats resumed.

The show goes on.

Only one witness saw what happened to Kaydy. The actress always did say it was easier to give her final soliloquy if she looked an audience member in the eye. And how lucky that person-of-the-performance was, she'd somewhat smugly thought, that they got to be part of the show – really, properly, *part* of the show.

So she'd watched a woman grow wings. She still had a scene to finish.

Her voice quivered, at first, and was rather quieter than it had been before. She stared up between the blinding stage lights, and the burn of them brought tears to her eyes. Later, she'd be complimented steadily to the bottom of one, two, three bottles of champagne split amongst her giddy-exhausted peers. She'd be told that tonight was her best performance yet. She'd unlocked something. Truly.

But, for now, she willed herself to forget. Forget who she was, and forget what she'd seen – because even artists, half the time, can never truly grasp the process. Only the product.

Applause thundered as the lights dimmed.

The actress stood child-frightened in the darkness, unsure of who to be between performance and final bows. She closed her eyes. She trembled, fixed in the terrifying midst of creation, waiting for someone to put the lights back up.

Jennifer McCormack
ALWAYS, SOMETHING IS LOST

When I was seven, my father started a new family. Three or so
months after my brother arrived, they moved to Yokohama in
Japan, where his new wife came from. I didn't see my father
much after that, at least, not until his recent return, fifteen
years later.

I have a full, reddish-brown beard now (I plan to maintain it
until my mother stops referring to it as my 'Taliban look'). On
reflection, this made me less immediately recognisable. I confess
that it was with cold satisfaction that I met the uncertainty that
registered on my father's face when I opened the door. Deciding
not to identify myself, I waited for him to seek confirmation.

He was divorced for a second time and missing his middle finger
on the left hand. I asked him if he was a yakuza. He laughed and
said he lost it chopping carrot batons. I preferred the less
domestic explanation, but then he said that I am 'just as imagi-
native'. I have never heard about this version of myself and I
must admit that I am curious to know more.

Together we have assembled,
a flatpack existence for him.

He is tired and glum, but voices no self-pity.

About five weeks ago, I suggested he get a dog, if his finances
would allow for that. He turned up the following day with a
golden retriever puppy. When I saw them walking together
down the driveway, it occurred to me that he had perhaps never
given major life decisions much consideration.

On the doorstep, he suggested I name the dog.

A consolation prize,
many years too late,
And besides,
I am the happy one,
now.

He said it was beyond him to name the dog. I made no mention
of the practice he'd put in (three brothers in all). We passed
some kids selling lemonade on the street, so I asked them for a
name. They suggested: 'Kanye'. Dad asked what I thought. I
arranged my face.

Not even my eyes were
windows to my inner
amusement arcade.

Like a presiding judge, I said: 'Kanye. Perfect.'

He also suggested we train the dog together. I looked at the
puppy. Could he be equally happy in control?

Always,
Something is lost,
Along the way.

And yet it was in this way that we went from being estranged to
co-parenting a puppy with an absurd name: a good dog, but
never better than when we both praised him for following an
instruction.

Today, we were at the beach, teaching Kanye not to swim out.
This was at my father's insistence. As a child he had witnessed an

old man screaming himself hoarse while his black Labrador swam out too far, into a troubled sea. He will never forget the anguish in this man's voice, dissipating into the crashing waves. There was nothing to be done, so my father's parents took him home. He didn't know what happened in the end. I imagine in some weeks or months he will, however, since there is really only one way such a story can end: we try to move on.

Rowan MacDonald
23 CLUB

Read aloud a psalm before each joint he smoked. Only fitting, since they were rolled with those Bible pages. Lady came up to him in the mall once, where he was hanging with other delinquent friends. 'You're doing good work,' she said, gently touched his arm, noticed the small Bible sticking out of his jeans pocket. He rolled an extra-large one that night, became so high people still talk about his telepathic abilities with animals. You should have seen this wallaby. It knew. They always do.

I first saw him cry when Amy Winehouse died. He wasn't even a fan; just felt she was a kindred spirit. He cried because she was dead at twenty-seven, had joined the Club, and he didn't think he would make that age. 'I don't have long,' he said.

He was always diagnosing himself with something new, some exotic disease, and used this as reason to do more drugs, more than the usual weed.

'Why don't you just see a doctor?' I asked.

I could tell I hit a nerve, triggered something. He said the GP asked more about his love life than his symptoms, and he got an awkward boner, couldn't be seen around there again. Laughed so hard I knocked over the jar of shrooms that was sitting on the coffee table, along with the homemade bongs created from Classic Chocolate Milks. He cried about this too, and I thought the Winehouse thing was getting a bit ridiculous, but then he gathered the mushrooms, sat with them in his lap.

'It's old Mabel next door,' he said. 'She had to get a new garden hose.'

*

He dated this chick, Stacey, tattoos up her arms, always wore Ugg boots, smoked Winfield Reds. Mabel said she was a good bird, that he should settle down with her. Poor bastard got emotional about this too, because he didn't want to be stuck with somebody who laughed at him, said he looked like *The Simpsons*, when he developed jaundice. I visited him in hospital during that stay. Brought him a Big Mac, because he said the hospital food wasn't fit for a dog.

'You've never had a dog,' I said.

'Fuck off,' he replied.

He enjoyed the Big Mac, tough seeing him yellow though. He pulled me close, whispered in my ear as I was leaving.

'Told you,' he said. 'Don't have long.'

He tried to off himself after the break-up, but wanted us to know it wasn't because of her. 'Got fired,' he said. 'No point anymore.'

Abattoir was sacking everyone, not just him; it went bust. He claimed the lack of free meat would make him anaemic now, and he was just cutting to the chase before it took hold. I mentioned this bloke, Angus, that I once served at The Bitter End.

'Has haemochromatosis,' I said. 'Donates blood to lower his iron.'

'Good for him,' he said. 'Probably never been sacked.'

*

It was a couple walking their dog early one morning that found him. Police cordoned off the beach, denied entry to others, even his mates. Surfers thought it was a drunk, perhaps one of their own, left him to sleep it off. When rolling waves started to drag him out, they figured something wasn't right. He would've been glad he wasn't yellow, didn't look like *The Simpsons*, when he died. More a blueish hue, like *The Smurfs*, which he enjoyed watching when smoking billies with the lads.

Funeral was held at the local community hall. 'Venue feels too large,' I said.

Mabel looked around at the small number of attendees. 'What a tragedy,' she sighed. 'He was a good boy.'

Stacey brought her new fella along, some biker with a tattoo up his neck, looked like he ate steroids for breakfast. Mabel saw this, bowed her head. 'Such a waste,' she muttered.

Towards the end, there was a PowerPoint presentation, with WordArt titles, as pictures of his life flew by to Green Day singing 'Good Riddance'. Celebrant then told us that he's now with the Lord, and I smiled, thinking all his Bible reading had paid off.

I went around to his place after the service, saw his mother packing his shit into boxes. She chucked it in the back of her wagon with the large dent across the passenger door.

'He would want you to have this,' she said, handing me a tin filled with weed; the good stuff he used to harvest out the back of Dover, where the tea-tree grew thick.

'Thanks.' I smiled, and we hugged, and I choked on patchouli, could feel her bony frame jabbing my torso.

It was Saturday night when I drove to the lookout, could hear the waves crashing ashore, same ones that engulfed his body that morning on the beach. I held the small Bible, tore out a page, started reading to anybody that would listen. Surrounding bushland chirped and squawked with animal sounds, mixed with sea breeze whistling through trees. Orange glow, deep breath. They knew. We all knew.

Crìsdean MacIlleBhàin

LITRICHEAN NAN LEUGHADAIR

(1)

'Cò leis na bhàirigeadh dhut dlighe binn
a thoirt a-mach air buill eile do theaghlaich
no ciont is lochd na paidhreach leis an tugadh
don t-saoghal thu a mheidheachadh air sgàlain

claoin do thuigse? 'G achdachadh gu stòlda
mar bhreitheamh 'na do shuidh' ann an taigh-chùirt
le cumhachd gun fhios ann cò às a fhuaradh?
Bu dhaoine meadhanach do phàrantan,

lag, fàillinneach, a rinn na b' urrainn dhaibh
gus d' àrach is d' oileanachadh, is tusa?
Bruidhnidh tu mar neach le tinneas-inntinn!'
'Dh'aithnich mi an t-olc 'nam phàiste fhathast.

Strì mi ris fad mo leanabachd 's 'na dèidh.
Ma chuireas mi an cèill gu pongail e
cha mhis' a-mhàin a bhios gam shàbhaladh.
Mas boile seo, 's e boile a chùm beò mi.'

(2)

An cnap-starradh bu mhoth' a thachair rium
san leabhar, b' e pearsantachd an ùghdair.
Abair *folie de grandeur*! Cò shaoileas tu
a th' annad, 's tu gad àrdachadh san ìr' seo?

Bheir thu binn is breitheanas a-mach
mar nach do choilean thu nad bheatha fhèin
mearachd, miastadh no suaraichead sam bith.
'S tu 'g iarraidh d' fhoghlam uil' a dhearbhadh, tha thu

toirt brath air leabhraichean 's sgrìobhadairean
nach aithne dhuinn, ag aithris ainmeannan
nach cuala neach nar measg air fad a bheatha.
'N aon chuspair agad, tillidh e gu stailceach –

do chudromachd, 's gach lochd a dh'fhuiling thu,
le bragaileachd 's co-thruacantas riut fhèin
a tha gad dhèanamh nas do-ghiùlain' fhathast.
Theab mi 'n leabhar a thilgeil chun na sgùilich.

(3)
Cà bheil an ceangal eadar Pasolini
's a' Ghàidhealtachd? Dè dh'fhaodadh sgrìobhadair
Eadailteach bhith teagasg dhuinn an Albainn?
An do lorg thu iomradh air a bheusan

no chlaonadh ann an dualchas nan Gàidheal?
B' eudar dhut facal gus a shònrachadh
a chùinneadh às ùr, bho nach eil aon athailt
mu ghiùlan air neo miannachadh dhen t-seòrsa

san tradisean a tha sinn 'g aithneachadh
's a' gleidheil. Gàidheal a' toirt pòig do Ghàidheal
eile? 'S a thuilleadh air seo, a' mealladh
is a' truailleadh nan deugairean, le bheachdan

cunnartach, sàrachail? B' fheàrr nan robh thu
coisrigeadh do thàlainnean is d' oidhirp
ris na tha dùthchasail, fìor-Ghàidhealach,
seach stealladh coimheach a thoirt do cholainn shlàin!

(4)

A Chrìsdein chòir! Na bi fo dhragh air sgàth
claonadh do mhianntan, no gad bhacadh ann
an dreachadh uile-eireachdas nan òigear.
Tuigidh sinn gur droch-ghnìomh bh' ann an sin

is tu nad bhalach no nad fhiùran, ach
dh'atharraich na beusan ann an Albainn.
Cha bhi ach dorlach mhinistearan no
bhodach a tha caisgte is claon-bhreitheach

a' coimhead air do shaor-chridheachd mar sgannal.
'S e fear-pòsta a th' annam, le triùir chloinne
a thaisbeanas gu seasmhach làn na tlachd
a bh' agam 's aig am màthair 's sinn gan gineamhainn.

Is àrd-aoibhneach an dreuchd ud. 'S e an aon
rud a th' anns a' ghaol 's an fheòlmhorachd
ge b' e na pearsannan as dèanadaiche.
Na bi fo iomagain, ach sàmhach. Sgrìobh!

(5)

Cha bhi na daoin' a' dannsadh ma tha iad
ag iarraidh àiteigin a ruighinn.
—Paul Valéry

Nan toirmisgte cleachdadh an fhacail 'mar',
rachadh bàrdachd Whyte gu lèir air ball
à sealladh. Chan eil e comasach air smuain
a leasachadh, a cheangal ann an slabhraidh

gus èifeachdan a mheasadh, is co-dhùnadh
fiach a ruighinn aig ceann a sheanachais.
An àite ceumnachadh air adhart gu dòigheil,
dìreach, stèidhichte mar shaighdear stòlda,

tulgaidh e an siud 's an seo mar dhannsair
beadarrach, aig a bheil barrachd cùraim
air camadh baogaideach nan gluasadan
's na pàtranan a tha gan eadar-fhighe

na air ceann-uidhe deireannach an tuairmeis.
Bidh mac-samhail daonnan ga bhuaireadh
mar chompanach san danns', an-còmhnaidh deas
ri threòrachadh gu plòigh cho-phàirtichte.

(6)
A Chrìsdein chòir! Tha lìonmhorachd nan cuspair
a nochdas fear seach fear nad dhàintean-sa
a' còrdadh rium, 's e do-dhèant' an ath sheòl
no 'n ath thionndadh a leanas a ro-innse.

Bha mi faireachdainn gum b' fheàrr nach robh mi
leughadh a' chruinneachaidh a-rèir nan àireamh,
nach robh mi tòiseachadh leis a' chiad duilleig
air neo crìochnachadh leis an tè mu dheireadh.

Dh'fhosgail mi an siud 's an seo do leabhar,
feuch ciod an stuth no 'n ìomhaigh ghlacadh m' aire,
air neo a spreigeadh mo chompàirteachas.
Is iomashlighe challaidean na dàintean

anns nach tèid duin' air chall. Faodaidh gach neach
na h-astaran innleachd as fheàrr leis fhèin,
no fantainn fhad 's a dh'iarras e air faondradh.
Mu dheireadh thall, buinidh an gàrradh dha.

(7)
Chan eil bàrdachd Whyte a' còrdadh rium.
A bharrachd air gum fàillig abaichead
'na smaointeannan 's 'na bheachdachadh, chan eil
aige ach aon argamaid – e fhèin!

An dèidh dhut duilleag seach duilleag a leughadh
mu gach sàrachadh 's masladh a fhuair e,
bhiodh dùil agad ri atharrachadh anns
a' ghleus, a' ghean no an dòigh-thaisbeanaidh –

cha chluinn thu ach an ceart ghuth gearanach,
chan fhaighear leat ach dearbhainnean gan aithris
a dh'fhàs thu sgìth dhiubh ranntan fad' air ais.
Abair creachadair nam faclairean!!

Far am fòghnadh buadhair geàrr is stuthail
bidh e a' cleachdadh dhà no trì, a' sireadh
cuideachd is taic bho ùghdaran neo-aithnicht'
's an cainnt cho doilleir, dubh ri a chainnt fhèin!

(8)
'S e comhairle a tha mi 'g iarraidh bhuat,
a Chrìsdein, on a tha m' fhear-gaoil 'na shagart
Caitligeach. Chan eil sin a' cur dragh orm.
Tha mi toirt urraim don fhuireachaileachd,

a' mhacantachd 's a' chùram leis am bi e
a' coileanadh a dhreuchd. Aidichidh mi –
is tu nad bhàrd, cha bhi naidheachd mar sin
'na h-adhbhar dèisinn a dhùisgeas gràin annad –

nach bi fàileadh na tùis 'na fhalt, no 'n smuain
gu robh na meòirean a bheanas ri m' chorp
'g aiseag an abhlain gu bilean nan creidmheach
gam mhì-thaitneadh. Chan eil a' chealgaireachd,

sìor-chòmhdach na fìrinn a' còrdadh rium.
Ach an rud as miosa, 's e mar a bhios e
ga chlaoidheadh fhèin, lèireadh buan a chogais,
milleadh a shlàinte. Dè bu chòir gun dèan sinn?

Christopher Whyte
READERS' LETTERS

(1)
'Who gave you the right to sit in judgement
on other members of your family,
to weigh the guilt, the crimes of two who brought you
into the world upon the biased scales

of your understanding? Or to proceed
like a judge, sitting calmly in a courtroom
with a power about whose source nobody knows?
Your parents were average people, weak

and fallible, who did the best they could
to rear and educate you. As for you?
You talk like someone who's gone off his head!'
'I got to know evil as a child

and struggled with it then and afterwards.
If I am able to describe it clearly,
I'm not the only one who can be saved.
This may be madness – but it kept me sane!'

(2)
The biggest difficulty I encountered
was the author's personality.
Talk about 'folie de grandeur'! Who do you
imagine you are, exalting yourself like that?

Handing out sentences and verdicts
as though you yourself never committed
a mistake or a base action in your life.
You're so keen to show off your erudition

you quote writers and texts nobody knows
repeating names not one of us has heard
mentioned at any stage in our lives,
and return stubbornly to your sole subject –

your own importance, and the wrongs you suffered,
filled with self-importance and self-pity.
That makes you even more unbearable.
I nearly threw your book into the dustbin.

(3)
Where's the connection between Pasolini and
the Highlands? What on earth can an Italian
writer have to teach us here in Scotland?
Have you ever come across a mention

of his customs or of his perversion
in Gaelic heritage? You have to coin
a new word for them, seeing not a trace
of similar desires or tendencies

is to be found in the tradition we
acknowledge and preserve. One Gael giving
another Gael a kiss? Corrupting
teenagers with nefarious, perilous

views? Better to devote your talent and
your efforts to what's genuinely Gaelic
and native, rather than injecting alien
elements into a healthy body!

(4)

Christopher, don't give in to concerns
about where your desires lead you, or stop
describing the full beauty of young men.
We know that when you were a boy or else

a teenager that was considered wrong
but here in Scotland things have changed since then.
Nobody but a clutch of ministers
or repressed people filled with prejudice

is going to be shocked at your openness.
I myself am married, with three children
who constantly remind us of the pleasure
my wife and I had in begetting them.

Sex is the height of joy. It makes no difference
what gender the two people involved are,
love and things carnal remain just the same.
Relax and set your worries aside. Write!!

(5)

Dancing isn't a way of getting somewhere.
—Paul Valéry

If they forbade the use of the word 'like',
everything that Whyte has ever written
would vanish. He's unable to develop
his thought, or else to link it in a chain

that measures its effects, so as to reach
a conclusion when his discussion ends.
Rather than proceeding on his way
like a soldier, sturdy and unswerving,

he rocks backwards and forwards like a giddy
dancer, more concerned with the capricious
wriggling of his gestures and the patterns
he's interweaving than he is with where

his hypothesis may lead him in the end.
He's constantly distracted by an image
like a dancing partner, ever ready
to have him as accomplice in a ploy.

(6)
Hi Christopher! The multiplicity of topics
you touch on in your poems, turn by turn,
appeals to me, as there's no way of guessing
beforehand what direction you will take.

I get the feeling it's better if I don't
read the whole collection from start to finish,
beginning with the first page, ending with
the very last. What I did instead was open

the book in different places, seeing what
subject or image captured my attention
or else aroused my interest and compassion.
Your poems are a labyrinth of hedges

where people don't get lost. Each must devise
their own specific way of travelling through
or else stay lost for as long as they choose.
In the end the garden will be theirs.

(7)

I just don't like Whyte's poetry. Besides
the fact his thought and his opinions lack
maturity, he cannot get beyond
one single topic – that's himself! When you

have read page upon page dealing with all
the injustice, the offences he has suffered,
you're justified in hoping for a change
of mood, a different tone or presentation –

the same complaining voice goes on and on,
nothing but truisms he keeps repeating
you grew tired of many lines before.
Talk about ransacking the dictionaries!

Where one choice and pithy adjective
could do the trick, he uses two or three,
seeking assistance from recondite authors
whose language is as baffling as his own!

(8)

I approach you in search of advice,
Christopher. My lover is a Catholic
priest. That's not the thing that bothers me.
I cannot help respecting the painstaking

gentleness, the care that he devotes
to fulfilling his duties. You're a poet –
which means that you're not going to be disgusted
or else indignant hearing me confess

that the reek of incense in his hair
and the idea the hands that touch my body
carried the host to the lips of the faithful
don't trouble me. I don't like the deception,

constantly having to conceal the truth.
The worst thing of all is watching how
he tortures himself, the damage to his health.
Tell me. What do you think we ought to do?

Translation by the author

Carol McKay
WATCHING ORION WHILE YOU SLEEP

Remember the days, the nights,
when all I wanted was to be with you?
I still do. But it's almost 5 a.m.

and I need the quiet of this empty living room,
this cardamom tea our daughter sent,
blue light from the modem
and posts from strangers on Instagram.

Above all, I need this clear sky view
of the dice toss of stars
that draw together as I watch
to form Orion.

There while I slept.
There, last week, obscured by clouds.
There all the times I never think of them.

Soon, there'll be daylight from the south-east
and I'll slip under the covers to be with you.
Tomorrow will be today. And I'll tell you
about the constancy of Orion, while I can.

PAWN

I found a chess piece on the paving slabs
under the lip of a rusting, cluttered skip.

Someone was having a house clearance
and scrapped it. Maybe they'd died. Maybe
they'd gone to seek a better life, in Spain,
or Vanuatu, or the Hasht Behesht Garden
in Isfahan's heart.

Maybe they'd finished an arts degree:
landed a job with a salary
of six-figures (now that's make-believe!)

or been jailed. It could be they found
true love: were borne away in the arms
of a good-looking man. I felt dizzy
when I bent to pick it up.

Not a king, queen, knight, rook or bishop.
A tiny treasure, small and insignificant,

carefully crafted in wood by a maker
unknown. I clutched it in my palm.

Gordon Mackie

WE WASTE AWAY LIKE SOMETHING ROTTEN

We left the party early, you ten feet ahead,
the straps of your dress bridling your shoulders,
me trailing behind, shirt clinging,
steam rising into the night.

When we got in, our hearts sank through the floor;
the living room had been visited upon
by a plague of moths. You gave me the look:
one of us had forgotten to shut the bathroom window.
The furniture pulsated with winged things,
a speckled blight on armchair and lamp shade,
while ensconced on the wall, appraising his flock
sat their high priest – a being the size of a small bird,
possessed of that precise mass at which we begin
to register a creature as another soul
sharing and puzzling over the planet with us.
His wings flickered like the pages of an old Bible
frantically seeking chapter and verse.

I grabbed a pint glass from the drainer –
the one I half-inched from *The Swan*
on your grandparents' anniversary –
and stamped it firmly to the wall,
quarantining him, the perfect fit,
and he strobed in the glass, bpm rising
as I handled him over to the door,
fancying myself as our resident bomb squad.
But when I reached the porch, removed my hand
and raised the glass to the darkness,
he did not thrash or flail or lose the plot,

he simply paused, suspended on the cusp,
batting his wings and flirting with the night
while his antennae traced the outlines of a question.

Then we watched through bloodshot eyes as he took off,
seeing him brush the dark surface of freedom
before the first stirrings of doubt took hold
and he fluttered back in through the bathroom window.

Jane McKie
WHEN WE STAY BY THE SEA WE DRINK ONLY WHITE STAR

The woman in the silver chair is rotating her ankle.
Around it goes; around it goes again

(repeat). A glass in her left hand from which
she, occasionally, sips. She is the picture

of wistful apart from her laugh, which makes the big
flowers on her black blouse vibrate, a belly

laugh – there – can you see them? The salmon-
pink overgrown hearts of them stuttering.

Later, where she sat, an abandoned pint of cider
flattens itself out. The colour of Lucozade,

it could be a feast for wasps if it wasn't
too windy, their probing, gluttonous bodies

buffeted from the deck, flicked like fag ends
at the bigger body of liquid waiting to drown them.

Iain MacRath
DHEIGHEADH SINN A DH'IASGACH

Dheigheadh sinn a dh'iasgach,
mi fhèin is m' athair,
is lìonadh sinn an eathar le
peilichean de rionnach, liutha,
is dheigheadh sinn timcheall a' bhaile
gu gach nàbaidh gus am biodh na peilichean falamh.
Chunnaic mi m' athair an raoir,
ged a chaochail e o chionn fichead bliadhna.
Chunnaic mi air na naidheachdan e
seacaid-teasairginn timcheall air
is an eathar làn,
làn de dhaoine.

Iain MacRae
WE'D GO FISHING

We'd go fishing,
me and my father,
and we'd fill the dinghy
with pails of mackerel, lythe,
and we'd go round the village
to each neighbour till each pail was empty.
I saw my father last night,
though he died some twenty years ago.
I saw him on the news
a safety jacket around him
and the dinghy full,
full of people.

Luke Mackle
CARLUKE

I heard mum scraping the toast downstairs. It must have been about the back of nine, as she's always leaving it too long in the grill when getting ready to go for the 31 bus down to my gran's in the morning. I heard her scraping it downstairs, heard the knife dropped into the metal sink, smelt the burn smell coming up the stairs to my room in the attic.

And then it disappeared. Not all at once, but gradually and irresistibly. The sound of a train having left the platform, gone now from sight, in the trees there, but its sound still present, coming back through the trees in a diminishing rumble then a whisper. And you on the platform, knowing that it has gone, knowing what it was that has gone, and you look down the tracks until they are consumed by hogweed and fennel and swarms of bees in summer sun until they then disappear and it goes still, the green recedes and the ground goes hard and cracked, and you see now that the platform has disappeared under an infinite Scotland sky and you are consumed in the void, and now it is the end of time itself and you at the end, looking back, waiting for the whisper of the train but it does not come, and all of this at once and the interminable slowness of February, of summers when young, of the moment the ball leaves the foot until it hits the net. The end begins in Carluke and there it ends, at the valley edge. I think how it will be hard to explain this to mum, blinking in the morning sunshine of May, listening to the scraping of the toast, hearing the knife being dropped into the sink, it playing out in a seasonable loop.

Outside there was a whisper of summer.

I lay still under the cool sheet and I looked at the square of blue through the skylight which just yesterday was black and low. I thought of the patio outside in the garden, the interlocking pink slabs with the moss in the joints. And of the grass, and how when I stood at the kitchen window a few weeks back it still looked silver and mottled in the close light and spring rain, and how it made me think of our old dog we had when I was wee. And I thought how the grass would look now in that May sun, how good and green it would look. And I thought of where the fields started at the end of the garden, through the wood lattice dad had fixed to the concrete where he'd grown his sweet peas. And through the diamonds in the lattice now the sweet peas withered, the light cut up and into the fields, and how they'd bend to the valley below Carluke. I thought of all this as I lay under the cool sheet.

Movement downstairs, I could hear and feel it. I could see it, as now I am in the garden and looking through the back window, mum at the sink, scraping the toast. I look down at my feet, bare in the grass, silver and white like the grass, it is no longer May. It may be February, a long, interminable February, but I am not sure if it is this one past or next. I can see the movement in the kitchen, the soft kitchen light, it is still dark out, it is morning and it is raining. I can see the movement in the kitchen, I can feel it all at once, blinking in the May sunshine here and feeling the fetid damp beneath my soles on the morning grass, it is happening all at once. I blink it out, I try and blink it out.

It is the first big weekend. I am lying under the cool sheet and I remember it is the first big weekend of summer. I listen to the clatter.

She has come up from London. It is the first big weekend of summer and that means it is the Scottish Cup Final. We will meet at the Electric Bar in Motherwell, and we will go from there to Hampden. I look at the blue sky as I lie under the cool sheet. Emma, James, Martin, Chick. We will meet at the Electric Bar, and I will tell her the idea I had for a book.

That sounds class, she says, she's not lost her accent but I've been saying she has even though I don't think it's true. Emma, she's come up from London. We are sitting on the picnic benches in front of the Electric Bar. James and Martin are chatting about something they'd seen on the internet and Chick is getting in

another round. I am telling her the idea, that a lassie takes a
job up north homeschooling two kids whose dad thinks they
are possessed with the devil and who spends his time trying to
communicate with his dead wife that he killed and buried in
the peat. *Fucking Calvinist*, she laughs. I am telling her this when
Chick comes back with the drinks and we get interrupted and it
doesn't feel right going back.

This all happens at once, the lying there and the conversation
with Emma, Chick getting the rounds, the others chatting shite,
the train to Central and the cans, the prick of worry in my chest
as I see the low fences and buildings with flat roofs pass by outside,
the trailing from the second minute until the eighty-fifth, when
the young boy on loan from Bolton leaves that big Hun bastard on
his arse and equalises, then minutes later scores again, to win. It
all happens at once, it is happening at once, the noise and eruption,
the disbelief, incredulity. Always bet against yourself, 'cause one
blow will always be softened. And I didn't this time. And I am
standing there celebrating, knowing that I have lost. Because lying
there under the cool sheet I remember taking it, the five hundred
quid mum had taken out the credit union to pay for her and my
gran's trip. I remember taking it, and putting it on us to lose. I
cannot remember why I did it, I must have had my reasons. We
were meant to lose, but we have won, and I have wretchedly lost.

I hear the bells of St Ninian's. The bells ring only on Sunday, and
so I realise it is Sunday, and that Saturday has gone. And I am gone.
I am dead because that was the choice I made, I made the choice
to go. But I have not gone, not really it seems, I am here under the
cool sheet, and downstairs mum is getting ready for mass. I hear
her scraping the toast.

This is where we are now, this is what has happened. I hear
footsteps on the stairs. Coming up the carpeted stairs, on the
landing and its white banister, and its photographs of me in school
uniforms, on the carpeted landing where I stood in school uniforms,
mum downstairs in the kitchen in the interminable mornings of

interminable Februarys. *Right Emma love,* my mum would say when she came round for me before school, *in you come now.* We sat in the front room, where the piano was, where the pictures were of my mum and dad even after he'd gone. We are sitting there with our tea and a bit of toast, outside is still dark and the yellow of the streetlamp bleeds through the sleet and condensation on the window.

In the corner of the room he is standing there, the May light on his face, which is featureless and white but textured and veined like basalt. *Some laugh, son,* he says.

A pause on the carpeted step.

There is a man who lives in a house at the end of a loch. I hear the crowd at the goal.

There is a man who lives in a house at the end of a loch. On one edge of the loch the water edge is all angled rock and impassible, lichen-covered and forgotten; east six to gale eight, increasing severe gale nine at times, moderate or rough, rough or very rough on the lichen-covered rock, the boat shed wet with showers, the visibility poor. The tops of the hills are hidden by low cloud and below them the heather and bracken are flat and brown and sodden. On the other edge of the loch is a village, but it is abandoned. On the cattle grate a half mile before the first house there is red paint which in broken letters says 'no'. There are a dozen houses, of which half have their slate roofs, the others being open and wild. In one where a fireplace used to be there is a neat pile of stones, and on the top stone lies a cross of heather.

A pause at the carpeted step, and I look to the basalt face staring at me from the corner. A bell at St Ninian's, and downstairs I hear the radio, a low tone of the waves. I am cool under the sheets because I have pissed myself, and I am lying in the wet sheets, and I say to myself, don't come in now, not yet. The voice on the stairs, it is my mum, she says *I told you to be up; Luke 17, things that cause sin will inevitably occur, woe to the person through whom they occur,* a pause; *put the oven on at twelve.* The steps turn and go down the stairs and a moment later the front door closes. The last bell rings. Ring a ding ding.

This is Scotland, I say to the basalt-face man, but he is gone. He is gone and I am alone, alone under the cool sheet, the May sun outside, warming. The end begins in Carluke and there it ends, at the valley edge. The fennel and the hogweed and the bees are there and then they are gone, and in the rutted field to the valley below I watch the seasons pass and go. Do not go there, I say to myself, do not go to the loch with the house at the end and the boat shed and the empty village. She does not know yet that I am gone but she will know and maybe now she knows and then she will go, I do not yet know why but she will go there, to the house at the end of the loch and the window with the light and the two young girls. I must tell her not to go, or tell her now to leave.

Some laugh right enough.

Emily Munro
FROG vs. PRINCE

The road was narrow, the sides not far apart.
There was room for one car, two bicycles, perhaps a van.
It was not such a distance to cross.
To the frog who needed to reach the marshes, who wanted to see
the water, who had an urge no person can articulate, whose
lungs were filled with singing air, the distance was unimportant.
The distance was too much.
Inside was bubble-gum.
The Jelly-Belly gumball smell dangled from the rear-view mirror.
Space infused with mall dreams, childhood longing,
syrup-covered ice shavings and girls on silver blades.
These desires were not far gone but insides are crushed quickly.
Frog spatter on the wheel. Brain along the stripe that divides the
road from field. That non-barrier where the grasses sway.
They nod and whisper.
Grow slowly through spring.
Stand sharp against the winter frost then wilt to start again.
The rains wash speckles of lung into the ditch.

The car drove while the sun shone and all the pieces of frog dried
up, were washed away.
The wheel was soaped in foam and the jellybean replaced.
The driver chose watermelon.
Watermelon sang of swimming days, of friendships in the year
of girlfriends with pale and naked stomachs, of crouching in
long grass, of feet inside the pond, of catching baby frogs and
their wishes.

TO START A FIRE

Bring sticks and oil, stack beneath a chair or bed.
Stay quiet. Strike a match or flip a lighter.
Feed a socket straw. Bring a candle from another room.

File away the cord on your father's electric razor. Fizz with
    bloody glory.
Then stand in abject fear. Run – you'd better. For your life.
Or don't. Don't run. Stay to watch, listen for sirens.

Hear your father's cough. Your siblings howl.
Watch polyester shrivel. Does nylon explode?
The TV melts.

Do I seem childish because I am 'occasionally enuretic'?
Does it matter if I am given to fantasy?
Will you hold me down?

Each look is a mark. We can play.
Who am I to you?

How to start a fire is: you make it in your head.

———

You're the one hiding. Where is my mother? Why did they hit me?
Who is my father? Why is my family?
A window, a screen.

A lock sharpens. Trees sway, their shadows scatter.
To be here is to drink water.
Your arms and the weight of the moon.

I'm live as a battery. If I were an orphan you could swing me
    from silk.
Apply gold to my skin. Arm my mouth and rectum with zinc.
Then when I die you can charge me with life.

Watch my fearful eyes shine.

Donald S. Murray
TALES OF A COSMIC-CROFTER

1
In his mind,
he'd harvest constellations
spread above his croft

where the moon could be a turnip,
purple-topped,
when it caught and reflected

the dying shade of sun,
changing to
a yellow swede at night-time,

when clouds would swell
and shroud its skin
with leaves,

while stars became a bright pail
of potatoes,
the Milky Way

grain scattered
round the black depths of the sky.
till he'd rise at midnight

and hitch his old, grey tractor
to the Plough,
churning over darkness

in the hope
next year would bring
greater store and plenty,

with crops and stacks
that stretched out
well beyond infinity.

2
He'd pride himself
at ploughing straight and fine

lines of longitude and latitude
upon his land,

not wavering in wind or storm
while he etched out

both tropic of Cancer,
Capricorn

upon his fields.
But he drew the line at the Equator

giving way to jungles
he might encounter there,

preferring the Arctic Circle
where he thought

his wheels could conquer
the ice he'd have to dig through

on a landscape
like his island,

bitter, windswept, bare.

3
Sitting in his capsule,
he stirs up the firmament,

his black wheels spinning
asteroids and comets

as he skirts the black hole
of a peatbog,

the bark of Canis Major,
shooting stars

that blazed and faded
in his youth.

He feels content to have stayed here,
fixed in his own orbit,

though there are times
he longs for

the company of cosmonauts,
some lifeline he might cling to

on nights when cosmic storms roll in
and he is forced

to plunge among distant planets
and step out from the shelter of his craft.

7

He found a clutch
with shells unbroken,
tucked within the Egg Nebula
below the Cygnet's wings,

and plucked them from their nest
to lie within the dark
brooding in his henhouse
until the night they hatched,

their yolks of light releasing
birds with feathers flaring
huge bouquets of constellations,
the glitter of far galaxies

men glimpsed and marvelled at
each time they passed
the corrugated iron shed
his flock of hens were caught and caged inside.

Sindhu Rajasekaran
UNREAL LOVE/R(S)

disclaimer: nothing happened

our love didn't betray; it didn't exist
except in my queer poems
of lusty longing licking her breasts &
when she sang crooked love songs
of cigarettes and other pop metaphors.
rhetoric vs. reality – in reality
we were mothers and wives
and proper persons.

but bodies yearn true

in alternate realities
across apps, sites, silence
chronotopes of desire
« thought of a thought »

wordless languages: codes of (mis)trust:
peak bisexuality: our love: tentative:
like a multilingual mirage

in Tamil, I lamented alone
so, she couldn't comprehend;
and often, she disappeared like a
maddah-allaidh, she-wolf, into the wild.
returned with a sharp knife

this is the end, she'd say
cut what's between us.
and I'd walk away,
bleeding.

spitefully I'd straight ignore her –
so foreign she was to me, but then I was
r/addicted, like on reddit
researching our stars, and I

got sad ^ mad
thinking of tears
fall from her green ocean eyes.

I wrote yet another Sapphic poem.
how can we end what hasn't yet begun?

like the dude on the horse that I was I
rode through the blazing winds
of social judgment
& gave her my words
of transgression

(then disappeared into my tower
transformed; now a longing veiled maiden)

till she fought the world's demons
and led her horse back to me,
and sang me another song,
in her handsome honey voice
strumming

« we looped a lot »

between us, we we/re
lover boys,

sweethearts,
        revolutionaries, poets,
nerds,
        nothing.

        nothing happened.

        yet the scars are real
        that knife
        her reckless rosyfingers
        cut me again

and now I know (. . .)

        in her musky scent
        spicy sweet, that time when
        my lips grazed her skin

        something happened.

Martin Raymond
THE PATH

I had uncovered the secret of life and death. Not an exclusive secret, for at the Post we all knew. You bent the envelope slightly, ran a thumb over the surface and held it just so, to the light. This allowed you to see, or maybe contrive, the faintest trace of the pencil lines on War Office form B.104. Pencil lines were drawn to cancel the terrors that didn't apply. The options were wounded, missing or killed in action. There was little solace in the first two, but at least they left some hope. We had quickly worked out where two lines close together meant only one dreadful outcome.

There was shame in the deed, although everyone did it. We were the custodians of many confidences across the parish and this was an intrusion into trust. Without discussion we had collectively resolved that to hand these letters over without knowing was worse.

I watched until Alexander had got the van into gear and it rattled and coughed towards Lochinver. Dust hung over the road. I shouldered my bag and set off down the track, out along the coast, the ancient, tiered sandstone mountains to my right, the sea to my left. I had the low sun at my back. I stood among the rocks and took the letter from my bag. It was like so many I had delivered. Buff and ordinary but containing multitudes. To hand it over was devastation. Is it blasphemous to say that these moments gave you an understanding of God? In an instant you created widows, orphans, crushed the future for mothers and fathers.

I took the envelope addressed to Donald MacIntyre Esq., The Lots, Achduart, and held it under the May sunshine. I smoothed the envelope with two thumbs. Two close parallel lines. In the wrong, or right, place. I felt the heat of the sun on my coat – the first real warmth of the year. I had spotted the letter when we sorted the mails last night, the others relieved that it was for my bag. They knew that it mattered to me. But I said nothing and I had said nothing at home. I wanted to be sure, and also, on the long five miles of the path ahead of me, I needed to hold onto the power of my knowledge, to have that glory to myself and feel its presence in my heart all the way to Mr MacIntyre's door. I would tell Sarah later.

The stones of the path clinked and rolled under my boots. Pollen from the heather dusted the cuffs of my trousers and I could smell the bog myrtle. I wasn't young, but I covered the ground efficiently. I was diligent, too. It's why I was given this route. So few dwellings and so easy for boys to take their time, make the most of being out of sight for all of the working day. That was when we had boys. They were all gone now. To France, to Mesopotamia, to the horrible grey swells of the North Atlantic. Some would return to their houses and crofts. But not to the ones where I had conferred my dark blessing.

I passed the old village, the stones hidden among the rising bracken save one suspended lintel, a door to nothing. Only in the heart of winter did the black stones show clearly. This was a sad landscape of loss where the past was as vivid as the present and memory endured like rock. It was not my land. I was from the south where there was no time to consider the ruins before they were built over, gone under a new road, a new row of houses. We came to escape the change and the noise, for a stillness. For the reeds pushing through the reflective waters of the peat pools. The wind in the chimney. That was our hope.

We were welcomed with a quiet politeness that served to keep us firmly at a distance. Even Grace. At school she was treated with courtesy and no suggestion of exclusion. Yet her friends were never close and though she did better with the language than her parents – it was not encouraged in the schoolroom but children pick up words almost without thinking – she was left with no one for her comfort when her world came to an end. No one beyond her parents, wracked with hurt and blind with fury.

The sea reflected the morning sky between here and the island, a drift of smoke from the sole house smudged across the pale blue. Where my path dipped down to the shore, Archibald MacNab was waiting, standing upright, the seaward oar in the water, the other shipped. It was so still I could hear the boat bumping the stones of the pier.

'Sin sibh fhèin,' he said.

'It is indeed, Mr MacNab. Though I have nothing for you this morning.'

He nodded then stowed the other oar. His eyes were lost under the shadow of his cap. Over his shoulder I could see the figure of Mrs MacNab framed in the doorway of the house. She had her hand flat above her eyes and at this distance her apron was a tiny flash of intense white.

'In this age lack of news is a thing to be cherished.' His English was spoken at a slower pace than his Gaelic, as if to make the point that this was a concession.

'We can't be held in judgement for what we carry on our backs. It is our burden,' I said.

His face showed all of his half-century of daily exposure to wind and rain and sun – the hard grappling with soil and wave. I sensed he had only distain for my employment. To be paid to walk was no occupation at all. This would never be said though.

'We all carry burdens.'

'I'm sorry you made the crossing for nothing.' I gestured towards the water.

'I cross like a blue-arsed fly every day.' There was no trace of humour in his face. 'I have nets to set over yonder.' He pointed to where the burn lost its way among the seaweed and sand of low tide.

'I'll let you get on,' I said.

A nod with his bunnet. 'Good day to you too.' He waved briefly to his wife. She turned into the doorway without waving back.

Their son had left for the sea decades ago and never returned. He was now with the Newfoundlanders in France. MacNab checked the moorings and was away across the beach towards where the half-submerged nets sagged between their poles.

As I followed the rising path MacNab's island opened up to me. The small fields, his two cows and scattered sheep beyond on the higher slopes. Isle Martin. Saint Martin's island, after an early missionary. The saint had been removed in the naming of it. No room for saints in the religion of this place. Yet the distilled Presbyterianism of the church was one of the few areas where I found a sense of connection when Sarah and I came here first, before Grace. Even though, or perhaps because, I understood not one word of the service and used my knowledge of scriptures to follow proceedings, I left the church every Sabbath with a peace that felt both comforting and steely. An austere confirmation of destiny drawn out of the wind and the salt skies that I could not explain, even to Sarah. In the end it was no consolation.

The path took me round the edge of the Ben, its slopes rearing above, higher in the early sun than under grey skies. I pushed on, hot now, to the point where the path squeezed over the shoulder of the headland, between rock and water. Here the world opened up, abruptly and totally. The islands and the sea in a blast of reflected light. On this calm day the light airs away out in the Minch had drawn great sweeping lines across the flat waters. There was the bristling distant speck of a warship and then the whispered smudge of the Hebrides and beyond that an Atlantic full of burning oil and dying sailors. We who carried the mails brought horror into this grandeur. Not that the sea or unpredictable stirks hadn't taken young men at other times. But accidents didn't need the apparatus of a chain of command, the War Office and an official letter to finish a family. Sarah and I had required neither war nor accident.

Beyond the shoulder the path began its course downhill, through the birchwood, full of broken light and layers of birdsong, and out into the croft lands. I drew in the scent of the birch sap as I left the last of the trees and took first sight of MacIntyre's house, its back turned. It faced the west and the sea, a sure sign of a recently built house with good windows and a wealthy owner.

The first croft along this stretch of the coast was Mrs Isabella MacLeod. She was out behind the squat croft house at her clothes lines. Two lines of four sheets hung limply. She was putting large wooden pegs to pillowcases on a third line. She took in washing from grander neighbours – including the MacIntyres. She could not make the croft support her now that she was on her own.

'A fine day for drying,' I said.

She turned to me as if surprised, though I knew I'd been visible for half a mile on the track since I'd left the woods. She took a peg from her mouth – it wasn't appropriate to be seen so casually by a stranger.

'There's no drying with no wind.' She put the wet pillowcases back in the basket and smoothed her hands down her apron. The apron looked as wet as the washing. Her hands were scarlet. She had the hesitant, distant manner of the bereaved, accentuated by my presence. She was a thoughtful woman, and did not, I'm sure, hold me responsible for the news I had brought over the last three years. But still, I had delivered death.

I handed over today's letter. With its censor's stamp it looked as benign as anything in a military envelope.

'It will be Findlay.' She made to put it into her damp pocket but thought better of it. She held the envelope by the corner.

'Is he still with the training ship in Southampton?' I'd brought Roderick's Admiralty letter after Jutland and Charles's on a foul November day late in Passchendaele.

'Yes.' She had the letter in two hands now. She wanted me gone.

'He will be safe there.'

'Dia na thoiseach.'

I nodded and put my arm through the strap of my bag. Over the tin roof of her house, out beyond the far islands, a bank of clouds was building to the west.

'And Grace? Do you hear from her?' she said.

'Nothing.'

'You still have her though.' She was still looking down at the letter.

'In a way, yes,' I said.

I think her intention was decent, her words true, although a living exile is a version of grief. I nodded again and walked round the house down to the path. No, there was no word of Grace, nor would there ever be since MacIntyre's son gave her a child and nothing else. In the iron laws of this place, a code I could not deny, she had to be turned away. Punished. We could have returned to the South, to the dirt of the city. But I was settled to the place and to the beauty of my given path. Through those awful years, daughter, granddaughter, wife, became estranged to me. Lost. Scattered. Isabella MacLeod knew this, they all did. And MacIntyre, wealthy on fish sent to the East, had nothing but contempt for us, for me. He was at the heart of our sorrow, his denials absolute, unquestioned by those for whom he was a man of respect. There was no justice. What were we to do, without family or connections or history here? Scatter too? But Sarah and I had clung on, silent, bonded in recrimination.

How easy to tell Mrs MacLeod that I carried in my bag the fracturing of MacIntyre's family. That in a life full of gain and evasion he would now know loss and face the irreconcilable. I walked on, the path looping towards the shore then up towards the MacIntyre house. My boots on the stones, the thumping of my heart and the ticking of the envelope in my bag all sang together. My belief was strong. There *was* a God who created mornings like this at time of strife. And a God who could balance hurt, make an equilibrium of grief. I would do no harm. I was a vessel for His will.

Alone in the parish, MacIntyre's home was reached by a track wide enough to turn a cart. All three storeys of the house rose above me. I slowed my walk. My arrival anywhere was of note, my timing predictable as fate, and I could bring comfort or despair. Pity the officer class. Unlike letter deliveries, a postman could approach with a telegram at any time. As soon as we were spotted on the road, or on a long gated drive, it was clear what we brought. But for the non-commissioned our arrival was neutral – until we handed over the envelope. If MacIntyre was watching my approach he would only see the father his son had wronged, a man haunted by the shade of a lost daughter.

I breathed deeply. The fresh salt air. No dung heaps round this fine house. I knocked and waited for MacIntyre.

The housekeeper appeared. Out of habit her eyes were narrow, defensive.

'Is Mr MacIntyre at home?' I took my time over his name. This was a moment. Seven years of desolation lay shored behind these few falling syllables.

'He is at his breakfast. I will take the mails.' She reached out.

I was ready for this. I was ready for him to have been out about his business. For him to be in Inverness. I was ready to return, to wait for as long as it took. I had prepared. Every step of every walk I'd taken down the shoreline path, every day from the outbreak of war, through his son signing for the Seaforths, each day, each footfall sharpened the thought of this possibility, of carrying this letter.

'I think, Mistress, that it would be better for me to give Mr MacIntyre his mails today.'

She turned away abruptly. He had several letters, postmarked Stornoway, Glasgow, Aberdeen, London. Business. I put the buff War Office letter on top.

He stood above me. A big man even without the three front steps. A linen napkin was tucked at his collar. I wasn't someone he had to arrange himself for. There were grease marks on the napkin, and for the first time I noticed the flecks of white in his beard. I held out the mails.

When he saw the envelope, he pulled the napkin from his neck and, as if it had nothing to do with him, let it flutter to the step. He took the small bundle from me. His eyes never left the top envelope. There was a tremor in his hand. I had nothing to say.

I walked his track back to the road. At the turn I glanced up towards the house. The door was still open. MacIntyre had gone; there was only a rectangle of black in the white house. There was no one at any window. The bright day was still high above me. Amen. I repeated it over in my head. Amen. In lieu of having any thoughts.

I was halfway to the next delivery when I heard him. It began with the roar of a bull in the slaughter shed and ended in the wail of a lost child. The sun had lit up one of the hill lochans on Horse Island. I walked on, feeling in my bag for the letters for the Mackenzie croft.

Aimee Elizabeth Skelton
ACROSS THE INNER SOUND

On the grass beside the newly unoccupied house, something has died. It's young and feathered and receded wide open, ribs covered in a sugar-like lice. 'Watch your feet when you get out,' Helen calls to her daughter, Jeannie, as she climbs out of the rental van.

'Ew, minging,' Jeannie says, sliding her feet down to the gravel.

'God, it's strange to be back after all these years,' Helen says. The house stands alone at the end of a short dirt path, just off the single road winding round the island's coast. It's coated in feather-grey pebbledash, with the only bright brushes of colour across the landscape the wooden doorframe – painted pillarbox-red some time ago, now patchy and peeling – and the old red telephone box in the front garden. It's gone so long now without a call that fern and fireweed sprout from inside, hot pink petals pushing up against the dirty glass panes of the door.

Up the hill from the house, a woman is taking her washing in off the line. She disappears momentarily behind the pillowcases, before unpegging them and reappearing again, taking the opportunity of the gap to stare down at Jeannie and Helen. 'Do you see that old wife up there?' Helen says, keeping her eyes fixed on the woman. 'She was living in that house the summer I came to stay here with Uncle Andrew, not long after he'd first moved up to the island.' Jeannie watches Helen's face as she speaks. Her mum's always been sparing in talking about the time she spent here. Helen breaks her gaze and slides open the back of the van, pulling out the two hastily packed bags with their clothes for the trip. 'I can't believe she's still going,' she says, half to herself. 'I doubt if she'd even recognise me now. Hardly bloody recognise myself these days!'

'What year was it you were here again?' Jeannie asks.

'Oh jings, donkeys years ago now. I would've been around about your age.'

Jeannie turns to look at the woman. By now, her line is empty, the washing basket full in her arms.

'Hello,' Helen calls over, raising her hand in a little wave.

The woman puts her basket down on the ground and makes her way over to them. Her skin – wind-beaten, threaded with purple veins – seems to age the closer she gets to them. 'Hello,' she says, unsmiling, straightening her butter-yellow apron flat. 'Are you lost?'

'Oh no, we're not lost,' Helen says, motioning towards the house. 'We're here to clear the house. Andrew was my uncle.'

'Oh. Right.' The woman's eyes move between each of their faces. 'Sorry for your loss.' Her eyes trail down at Jeannie's right arm, tattooed with moons in various waxing phases. 'I never knew he had family to be honest with you. Never really knew that much about the man at all.'

'Me neither, in the end,' Helen replies. She rummages through her handbag, retrieving a cigarette from a half-empty twenty deck. The wind spits against the lighter's thin flame as she tries to light it. Once its lit, she takes a long draw and exhales. 'I was close with him when I was younger, I actually came to stay here one summer in the early nineties.'

'Oh aye? Come to think of it, you do look familiar,' the woman says. 'Correct me if I'm wrong – was it yourself and another woman?'

'Aye – I was with a friend.' In all the times Helen's spoken to Jeannie about her time on the island, she never mentioned coming with a friend. Jeannie looks down at her hands, starts picking at a strand of skin on her thumb. 'Anyway,' Helen continues, 'my mum and Andrew stopped speaking around that time. They never quite saw eye-to-eye, you know how families can be. It wasn't long after that I got pregnant with this one here.'

'I hope you don't mind me saying,' the woman says, after a short pause, 'but I did always think of Andrew as a bit *queer*.'

It's the first time Jeannie's heard the word used like this – in its stale old form. It hangs around in the air between them like damp. Neither Helen nor Jeannie reply, but the woman doesn't seem to take much notice. Her eyes – almost hidden under a tired hood of skin – have wandered from Helen's towards the cottage window behind them, ageing the filth lines, identifying the silhouettes. The curtains, made from a thin white mesh and trimmed with floral lace, are drawn closed.

When Jeannie lived at home, Helen would bite her head off if she left the curtains closed through the day, saying everyone in the street would think they'd died, or worse, that they were living as good as dead. When she moved away to begin the first of her three unfinished degrees – sculpture at the art school – she rarely ever opened her curtains.

'The house'll be an awful job for the two of you to do on your own will it not?' The woman says, without taking her eyes away from the window. 'You'll let me know if you're needing a hand?'

'Oh you're very kind,' Helen says. Jeannie glances at her mum, trying not to let the horror show on her face. 'Anyway, we better be getting ourselves in and settled before it gets dark. It's been so nice to meet you—' she pauses, unsure how to address the woman.

'—Christine,' the woman replies, bringing her palm to her chest. A gold wedding band sinks into the tough, purple skin of her ring finger.

'Helen,' Helen returns. 'And this is Jeannie, my daughter.' She motions towards Jeannie with the lit cigarette.

As Christine heads back up the garden path, Helen fumbles with the set of keys she was given at the council offices by a skinny man in glasses who looked about twelve. He talked them through the terms of the house clearance in a Hebridean accent, his voice at times sounding as though he was drifting into light song.

'You have a total of fourteen days from the Monday following the deceased relative's death to clear the property. This time period is free of charge,' he'd told them. He looked up from his computer screen briefly. 'Of course, we're on Thursday now, so you only have a total of eleven days left.' He returned to the screen. 'You are expected to clear all items from the property. This includes furniture, personal belongings and furnishings such as floor coverings. If, for whatever reason, you need more time to clear the property, you will be charged according to the weekly rental rate until the date when you are able to return the keys.' He scribbled a phone number on to a pink post-it note and handed it to Helen. 'This is my Uncle Jim's number. He can help you get rid of any unwanted furniture items or rubbish.' He leaned back in his chair and drummed his fingertips on the table – his fingernails bitten right down to the nail beds.

Inside the house, a layer of dust settles across the surfaces. Along the window sills, found objects from the island have been placed. A chalky piece of driftwood, a collection of feathers standing upright in a crinkle-cut beetroot jar, the solid body of a starfish, the tiny white skull of an unknown bird. The floorboards creak under their feet as they make their way to the living room. A map of the island papers the wall, the land printed in gradients of greens to browns. It's been annotated like the pages of a used book – circles drawn in black ink along the meandering coastline, words scrawled in tiny, illegible lettering. Saucers and ramekins overflowing with ash and cigarette butts balance on the arms of the couches.

'Christ almighty, you could stir this place with a bloody stick!' Helen says. 'I'll no be asking that Christine over to give us a hand, I'll tell you that for nothing.'

Exhausted from travelling up from London that day, Jeannie decides to get herself ready for bed early. She runs a brush through her dark hair, plucking out the single spiralling grey that keeps appearing in her parting with her thumb and index finger. A single plastic toothbrush lies on the side of the sink. In the bathroom cabinet, a packet of ibuprofen with two pills left in the blister pack, a half-empty bottle of 3-in-1 shower gel, cotton buds, a disposable razor with grey fuzz congealed between the blades, a bottle of TCP. Jeannie finds herself wondering why her mum didn't opt for the council to clear the house, why she'd insisted on travelling the whole eight-hour journey to sort through his belongings with her own hands. She expected there to be more valuables or sentimental objects, but so far, the house seems disappointing in its ordinariness.

When she comes downstairs to say goodnight, Helen is sitting down on her knees with her back to the door, a pile of paperwork and photographs pulled from the wooden cabinet in front of her. She's holding a letter that looks to have spent so many years folded in quarters. It now hangs limp in her hands like a sick bird. She doesn't notice her daughter's presence. Jeannie always feels the most connection to her mum in moments like these when she's alone, and not in her role as teacher, or mother, or wife. Since retiring from the high school where she worked for twenty years, Jeannie's noticed this version of her slip through more and more often.

'That's me off to bed, Mum,' she says finally.

Helen jumps. 'Oh, hen, I didn't realise you were there.' She folds the letter back up and slides it into the pile. 'I thought I might as well get started on this tonight, I'm still high as a kite from all the tea on the road up.' She turns her head back to the paperwork. 'Hope you get a good night's sleep.'

Jeannie takes the opportunity of the distance between them to ask about something that's been circling her mind since their interaction with Christine. 'Who was the friend you came here with when you stayed with Uncle Andrew? I always thought you'd come alone.'

Helen keeps her back turned, palms resting on top of her thighs. 'Her name was Sam. We met during our teacher training.'

'Do you still speak to her?'

'No. We lost touch.' She starts to sift through the pile again, tossing unopened bills to the side.

That night, Jeannie drifts from dream to dream. In one, she's hours late for something important, lost and moving slowly across an unfamiliar city with a quiet sense of dread. In another, she's pregnant, with no memory of how it'd happened. The pregnancy manifests in eggs growing in translucent jellied clusters under newly grown, enormous breasts.

When she wakes, her heart's quickened. An acidic vomit feeling rises up from her chest to her throat. She checks her phone. 5:43 a.m. Still no signal. The room is already full of an unsure daylight. She decides to get some air, and heads downstairs to put her coat and shoes on.

When she gets outside, the air is completely silent, as if the water has sucked the sound down into its dark belly. Jeannie reaches the peeling gate at the bottom of the garden path. The grass beneath it has been left to sprout so wildly that she has to tug for it to open just a fraction. She walks down the machair and on to the beach, feeling dried seaweed crackle and pop underfoot. Every so often, she steps around the debris brought in by the tide – milky jellyfish bodies lounging in dramatic poses, seabirds on their backs with their eyes closed as though they'd fallen from flight mid-dream.

The island seems to be littered with bones. Baby-toothed skulls nesting in the machair, cartoonish femurs shining white under water, licked clean by the tide. She's surprised to not be creeped out by any of it. Not the mud wedged between the teeth in the lamb skull, nor the question of where the rest of the bodies must've gone. They feel more like seashells if anything – structures that once homed, now decorating.

She remembers reading somewhere about the island's animals, many brought over as a part of research – herds of miniature brown sheep, tall goats with wild, spiralling horns and wry smiles, wild horses with white, speckled coats only ever seen far in the distance before scattering. The studies are long-finished now, the findings lying dormant in academic search engines waiting to be dredged up whenever the nature of the animals' lives become relevant.

Jeannie's phone starts to vibrate in her pocket over and over. She unlocks the screen and watches notifications drop down from her news app, one after another as if they can't catch a breath.

Mass Evacuations Across the Med as Wildfires Rage. Gulf Stream on Brink of Collapse. Politicians Using AI to Write Manifestos. UK Grants Hundreds of New North Sea Oil and Gas Licenses. Fifty Bidders Per Rental Property as Prices Soar.

The hospitality agency she works for ad hoc in London have sent twelve generic requests for staff. Jeannie's eyes scan across them: a wine waiter for a party in a private home in South Kensington, a cloakroom attendant for an executives' dinner at the Science Museum.

On Instagram, a friend has sent a meme of a kitten swaddled in a blanket with the text *can't mistakey if not awakey*, along with an article entitled *The Kids Are Not Kids Anymore,* asking why millennials can't commit to responsibility. Jeannie skim-reads, scrolling past intermittent ads for a one-pound sale on Shein bikinis. *Freedom is marketed to us in a trade-off for responsibility*, the writer writes.

She finally resorts to Hinge, where she's acquired various matches since the time she last had data. Hamish, a DJ from Edinburgh, states his irrational fear as 'forgetting to take the gherkins out a Big Mac'. Jeannie responds out loud, 'clearly you've never had dreams about frogspawn growing under your massive tits, Hamish,' as she swipes through dimly lit photographs of him behind DJ booths. Her second match is Lucia, a translator from Galicia. Jeannie looks at their eyes in the photos they've chosen, as she always does, searching for a familiar knowing. She closes the apps, locks her phone and slips it back into her pocket. At that moment, she notices the incoming tide has been lapping at her shoes, now soaked through.

She moves back up towards the machair, starting to notice signs of life left like track marks – a flattened path formed under feet in the overgrown bracken, an empty half-bottle of Bell's whisky, a shattered snail shell – crunched into five sharp parts. She wonders if any of it was the doing of her great-uncle Andrew, in the days before he died.

The house is still in silence when she gets back. On her way to the stairs, she notices two neat stacks of papers on the living room floor, where her mum was sitting the night before. Kneeling down beside them, she sifts through the paper with her fingertips. In the middle of the pile beneath her right hand, she finds the folded letter – the paper so soft it could fall apart in her hands.

George Smith
WILD FLOWERS

Startit a couple ae years back. Jist a whisper in thi darkness.
Best not leave a belt in the bedroom.
Lyin in ma pit it night-time. Jist a fuckin whisper.
Best not leave a belt in the bedroom.
Every night. A horrible fuckin whisper. No even a formed character.
Best not leave a belt in the bedroom.
Jist a whisper.
Eftir a couple ae months ae whisperin, it startit tryin tae annex ma face durin thi night. Then – it right upped thi ante wae its land grab n startit makin advances in thi mornins tae.
Bit – is time passed – Ah goat tae know thi snooty cunt. Aye – thi snooty cunt. Turns oot – it wisnae an it – it wis a fuckin him. A whisperin fuckin parasite.
Ah've wan slight advantage though. Ah'm workin class – unlike Lord Tingly Fuck Face – thi Duke ae Auld Pile. Meanin – Ah'm usually up afore thi lazy landed bastart.
Ah lie in ma pit fur a glorious five minutes. No a wurd fae thi cunt. Silence. Nada. Nantae. Mibbie ees no comin thi day? Mibbie ees died? Mibbie ees shaggin wee weans? Mibbie – since Ah've a minute – Ah should introduce masel. Ah'm Harry Williams. Nice tae meet yae.
Naw. Naw. Naw. Thi bastart stirs. Ah see im in ees silk gown – sprawlin oan ees four poster bed. Ee reaches fur thi servant's bell – restin oan ees African Blackwood bedside cabinet. Long bony fing-ers lazily ring-ring-ring n ma face starts ting-ting-ting n thi fuckin tinglin begins fur thi day. Then ee starts.
Best not leave a belt in the bedroom. Best not leave a . . .
Fuck you – Lord Tingly Fuck Face – Ah shout.
No. No. Fuck you oink, he replies.

Naw. Fuck you – ya toffy fuckin cunt.

Sooty Rabble. Fucking Hoi Polloi, he hisses back. Thon bell ae his is ma cue tae get up. Ah stagger intae thi cludgie. Problem is – Ah'm no sure if thi posh cunt's even real. Ee might actually be part ae ma ain face. Bit – it thi same time ees thi realest cunt Ah've ever met. Lookin it im in thi mirror Ah sais – Tellin yae ya cunt – me n you ur gettin divorced. Ah'm fuckin sick ae yae. Ee jist sneers back it me. Truth be tolt – ee's probably sick ae me tae.

Pointin it im – Ah scream – Ah'll dae ma hing n you kin dae yours.

You're not getting rid of me that easily, he says.

Ah sais – huv Ah no been good tae yae?

Not really, he smirks.

Yer no even good lookin ya cunt – Ah tell im.

You should have taken better care of me, he chirps.

Ah draw im a dirty look in thi gless. How did it come tae this?

*

Well – as Ah said it startit a couple ae years back. Ma face startit tinglin n burnin n reddenin n tightenin. Sometimes ma nose wid drip. Others – Ah felt awh blocked up. When it goat really bad – like it is this mornin – felt like ma ears wur leakin n ma brain wis drippin doon thi inside ae ma face. Jist fuckin weird. Then this posh cunt startit talkin tae me. Fuckin oan n oan – awh night – every night n then awh day – every day. That's no even thi weirdest hing. Tellin yae thi weirdest fuckin hing wis dealin wae thi doakters. First doakter tellt me oor thi phone thit it might be Rosacea – never even seen ma face. Never even examined me – thi fuckin giraffeaquack. Second doakter tellt me it might be Trianimal Neuralgia n gied me anti-D's. Tellt im Ah wisnae takin thum – Ah'd been vegetarian fur years. Doakter eftir that tellt me it wis a sinus infection n gied me antibiotics. Then – Ah ended up in thi Death Star – Glesga's newest hoaspital.

In thi hoaspital – posh cunt piped up in ees toffiest tones.
A private room on the NHS. A waste of good resources.
Ee wis burstin ma fuckin chops.
I'd have sixteen of you swine on an open ward.
Then ee wis away again.
George Orwell wrote in his final diary entry that everybody gets the face they deserve by the time they are fifty. You must have been a nasty little oik. Probably slit your master's throat.
Never shagged ma sister though.
Half-sister, he insisted.
Ah wis lyin oan thi bed – wishin Ah hud a therapy cat. Fuckin hate cats tae. Much rather huv hud a therapy dug – bit it that point a therapy cat sounded awhright in comparison tae thi Duke. Jist sommit tae huv stroked. Taken ma mind aff thi cunt. Fuck it – Ah thought – Ah'm away fur a shower. Ah dreepied aff thi bed n carefully guided ma roller drip staun tae thi shower room.
An en-suite bathroom?
Thi sarcasm wis drippin frae thi corners ae ees mooth n ee wis shakin ees heid in disgust.
Needed tae get rid ae thi cunt fur ah wee while. So – Ah part stripped oot ma goonie – leavin thi drip airm covered – walked intae thi shower n startit singin tae droon im oot. That's when thi resistance movement startit.
Durin ma time in thi hoaspital – Ah even tweeted @allygreyman – a well-known land reformer – n begged im tae help me wae a community buy back fur ma dial. Ee totally fuckin blanked me – bit. Probably thought Ah wis aff ma face.

*

Anyway – back in thi cludgie – thi noo – Ah'm brushin ma nashers n thi cunts away again.
Oh, your teeth are awful.

Wanker.

                  I know a good joke on the theme.

Prick.

                      Would you like to hear it?

No really. Ee ignores me n kerries oan.

             Doctor. Doctor. Can you help me with my
yellow teeth?

Lea me in peace.

            Yes, sir, indeed I can. I prescribe a brown tie.

Ah rinse n spit – then jump in thi shower tae rid masel ae thi
crazy cunt. Under thi hose – Ah run through thi resistance juke
boax. Aye – this'll dae. Ee fuckin hates this wan. N it's perfect fur
thi shower tae. Bubbles ya cunt – Ah shout. That'll fuckin shut
yae up. N Ah let it rip.

MJ's fur ever blowin Bubbles – Monkey spunk everywhere –
blown in thi bath – man yer huvin a laugh – doon in Neverland
– bastart's boat a Giraffe. Monkey's always smilin – cause MJ's
always there – MJ's fur ever blowin Bubbles – Monkey spunk in
thi air. West-Ham!

                      *

Eftir ma shower, Ah'm doon stairs, it the kitchen table, drinkin ma
mornin cuppa n speakin tae ma generals.

Ur we winnin this war? Ah ask thum bluntly.

It's awh lookin intae space n dodgin thi question afore General
Williams picks up thi bit. Tae be honest wae yae – Harry – it's nae
good. Thi Duke ae Auld Pile – Thi Duke ae Hamneggilton n awh
these other aristocratic cunts ur haudin maist ae thi land in thi
country. N as yae know well enough – Auld Pile n ees troops ur
makin steady headway intae yer face n there seems tae be fuck
awh we kin dae tae halt ees advance.

Ah nod in agreement wae ees assessment. Then ee pipes up wae
a suggestion.

Thi runnin may be oor only chance tae drive thi bastarts back. Ah know yer knees ur fucked wae the fitba – Harry – bit it's goat tae be worth a try.

    This should be entertaining, Auld Pile sniggers.

Ah blank thi cunt n decide that Ah'll follow Williams's advice – wance ma work's done fur thi day.

*

Eftir a day's graft – where thi cunts never left me in peace – Ah'm doon oan thi Clydebank Riviera n Ah'm runnin fur victory. Well – fuckin hobblin fur victory. Ah gingerly cover aboot hauf a mile in absolute silence afore thi cunt starts, n ma chist caves in.

    You look like the tin man.

Fuck off.

    I've some four-stroke oil in one of the outhouses.

Arsehole.

    Shall I have John Grant retrieve it?

Gie me fuckin peace.

Eftir another hauf mile ae ees shite – Ah'm blowin it oot ma erse – n ee delivers a devastatin blow.

    Why is your left hand tucked into your side?

Whit?

    Passers-by may think you're a stroke victim.

Ees goat a point thi cunt. N as Ah hobble oan – thi gaps atween ees chunterin get even wee-er n wee-er.

    This can't be considered running. Nothing but farcical.

Gie me fuckin strength.

    You'll not even live to be sixty-three.

Ah jack it fur thi night. Bit – Ah think we might be ontae sommit.

*

Eftir ma run – Ma heid's bangin n ma face is tinglin like fuck. It's jist fuckin horrible. So – Ah decide tae huv a bath.

Under thi wah-tir – Ah'm thinkin – mibbie a could droon thi cunt.

You can't kill me without killing yourself, he asserts.

Ees bang on – thi snooty fuck.

Think rationally, he implores.

Bit thur's a worried tone in ees voice.

Thur's fuckin millions ae us n only a few ae youse cunts. Whit's tae stoap me? Ah asks.

The law for one thing.

Thi law?

The law in this country protects my rights.

Your rights?

It was constructed with this principal in mind.

Fuckin valid point – thi cunt.

Whit if thi law's morally bankrupt? Ah ask im.

You're not above the law. Impudent swine.

You've nae right tae ma face ur any other land – ya cunt. Yease fuckin stole it n took it bae force.

No. No. we're the lawful custodians of the land.

Very fuckin good.

Her rightful protectors.

Yer fuckin hoop.

While Ah'm it ma dinner – Ah consider further.

*

Later – ees pish is that bad – Ah'm forced tae make a retreat fur ma scratcher. Lyin in ma pit – Ah try tae meditate – bit – oan n oan n oan ee goes like some aristo fuckin Krishna in a trance.

Best not leave a belt in the bedroom.

Shut it.

Best not leave a belt in the bedroom.

Fuckin shut it.

Best not leave a belt in the bedroom.

Ya fuckin parasite.

Bit naw – does ee fuck. Ees posh parasitic mantra rings through ma nut n ma face is fuckin dripping fae thi inside oot. Fuckin plastic bag oan an open fire. Thi fuckin tinglin n ees horrible whiny voice ur fuckin drivin me tae despair.

Best not leave a belt in the bedroom.

Kill im.

Your sort just don't have the gumption.

Yae think?

Best not leave a belt in the bedroom.

Kill im.

Nor the wherewithal.

Seriously?

Best not leave a belt in the bedroom.

Kill im.

Nor the capacity.

Is that right – ya cunt?

You'll not carry it through.

Jist ae matter ae logistics.

You'll never do it.

Door haunle or bed frame?

Best not, he pleads.

Lamppost oan thi street's a bigger statement.

I'll have recourse to the law.

Ah um thi fuckin law.

Take my trinkets. But, leave me my house and my land.

Your land? Ah wahnt ma fuckin face back. Ah'm takin thi fuckin lot. Trinkets – thi hoose n thi fuckin land. Thi whole fuckin kit n caboodle. This is ma fuckin land. This is ma fuckin face. N you've taken enough fur too fuckin long.

No. No. No, he begs.

Drawin a belt fae under ma pilla – Ah string im up tae thi bed frame.

This is a mistake.

Favourite belt.

                                        This is insane.

Fearful eyes reflected in thi silver cowboy buckle.

                            No. No. No.

Small details.

                                Have mercy.

Faded brown leather.

                          In the name of God, man.

Ees struggle fur breath.

                              Godless oaf.

Wild flower etchings.

                      My titles.

Thi kicks.

                      My castles.

Thi magnificent seven buckle holes.

                      My estates.

Thi jerks.

                          My.

Thi girl who bought it.

              My.

Thi sting ae ees tears streamin doon ma face.

           My.

Thi quiet.

Morag Smith
RENAISSANCE BAT

*(From a watercolour, circa 1790, Asian Lesser False
Vampire)*

Beneath a Mona Lisa smile you're splayed
for pinning. I recall the callipered
shadow of Vitruvian Man, from caverns
and hollowed trees to this small page.
Notice the artist's worship of your thumb-claws
– they hold up sails of wings that can make
the air water for swimming in. Deep time
echoes in those downy caves of ears.
We drew pyramids and squares, you listened,
carried the pox for fifty million years,
ate our locust plagues and held within
your matchstick bones what's near forgotten:
that God's an insectivorous vertebrate
thirty-four grammes in weight.

Caitlin Stobie
DEEP DIVE

1.

It's May and I am running. I run because I'm not sure if it's safe to swim here – here being Newhaven, my home, a few miles north of Edinburgh's city centre. Newhaven was a fishing village from the 1500s until the 1950s. In this harbour, fishwives in great striped aprons used to pick mussels and haul creels on their backs. They'd carry up to fifteen stone of fish right uphill to the city where, for just as many miles, they'd sell their wares from door to door. Sometimes, they'd take their baskets onto trams and buses and ruin others' journeys with the stink of fish. I run with my earphones in and listen to Japanese Breakfast, a band fronted by Korean American writer Michelle Zauner. I mouth the lyrics to 'Diving Woman', a song about the haenyeo, the real-life mermaids of South Korea. The women of Jeju Island have trained themselves for generations to deep-sea dive without an oxygen supply, holding their breath for up to three minutes to harvest molluscs and seaweed. *I want to be a woman of regimen*, Zauner sings. *I want it all.*

Here in Newhaven, I wonder how many strong seawomen wandered along these very cobbles. I pass the redeveloped stairs on Main Street where, just like the haenyeo, women would mend and bait their men's fishing lines. I say 'their men', but Edinburgh's fishwives weren't necessarily married. If they were, their opinions mattered far more than other women's of the time – another quality they share with Korea's diving women. History books call their world a 'gynecocracy', a political system run by women, but it seems more complex to me. The fishwives of Newhaven were described as both beautiful and brash. They took on domestic and physical labour, working with and for men who arguably did far less, but there was also something manly about them: they swore profusely, leading to the phrase, 'a tongue like a fishwife'. If a man died at sea, then his wife would often take over the business – as was the case with Maggie Noble, whose husband contracted an illness while fishing in South Africa in 1933. Like the haenyeo, the women's duties lay somewhere between the gendered worlds of home and commerce, land and sea.

While there are still diving women on Jeju Island today, most of them are over the age of fifty. Newhaven's fishwife population started to decline in the mid-twentieth century; the last woman, Esther Liston, retired in 1976. The Firth's native oysters went extinct around the same time within a related mesh of reasons. The industrial revolution had led to poor water quality: chemicals from textile factories, paper mills, and coal washing plants all bled into the water. Edinburgh's untreated sewage was pumped straight into the Firth until 1978, when the Seafield Waste Water Treatment Works was constructed just next to Portobello, a popular swimming beach. Together with the sewage works, EU legislation helped to improve water quality – but the UK has since left the EU and the oysters remain extinct.

2.

In her book *The Second Body*, Daisy Hildyard outlines how all humans beings have two bodies. The first is the fleshy cage, that one that reads and listens and swims. The second is something more abstract. It's the knock-on effect of every decision that our urging bodies have ever made: the screams and faeces of the pigs you eat, the jet fuel fumes behind my imported kimchi. I alternate between believing in this second organism and feeling like I've never really held much power over the fate of my own body, let alone others'. Sometimes, I am too tired for a deep dive.

Yet diving – real diving – is also what makes my body sing. Descended from Irish and Scottish immigrants, I grew up in the '90s, swimming in South Africa's streams and oceans. Indoor pools are wasted on me and it's not that I swim to keep fit – or rather, not only. I like lying in the sun and reading a book until I am sick with words. Then I do a slow breaststroke interrupted every few minutes by plunging deep, deep, until my lungs and head are dense with primordial cold. Water is a cure for feeling too, well, human. That's what it is to be immersed, truly.

Some days I do head east to Portobello, but the Scottish Environment Protection Agency warns not to swim there for up to two days after heavy rain because of overspills. Other times I walk west to Wardie Bay, which has just been designated as Scottish bathing water for 2023 – though it isn't yet on the Safer Seas & Rivers app. My friends and I bask in the unseasonal sun but still gasp at cold shock when we put our heads under. We look out for metres-long tentacles of lion's mane, a stinging red jellyfish that only appears in the warmer months – which are the only months we want to swim, too. Then I see a map of storm overflows on BBC News and the entire nation of Scotland is mysteriously whited out. I hear a rumour about a seal carcass being spotted in the harbour. So, for a spell, like today, I run, instead. I do not like to run. My breath catches in my chest and I'm quick to get shin splints or otherwise injure my legs – but unclear water scares me.

Wild swimming's growing popularity has brought awareness about the dumping of raw sewage in British waterways. The people of Edinburgh North and Leith, who voted overwhelmingly to remain in the UK, blame Brexit. Of course politics plays a role, but the problem is bigger than one party's poor decisions. What shocks people here is no news for developing countries. South Africa is one of fifty-one states to be part of the Blue Flag awards for pure water and clean coasts. Countries must volunteer for their beaches to be considered for Blue Flag status (while England, Ireland and Wales participate, Scotland does not). South Africa's beach stand-ards vary dramatically. In Durban, near where I was born, not a single beach qualified for a Blue Flag in 2023. When I went to visit family for the first time since the pandemic, I was impatient to float in the Indian Ocean – but there was severe contamination from overflowing sewage treatment works. Still, after two years of British weather, I was desperate. I hiked inland to a remote stream pool where my mother once contracted Bilharzia. The water was clear and gushing and at the falls I was pulled under, head completely immersed, and in that moment I don't know if I was more scared of *E. coli* or freshwater snails. Untouched wilderness has its risks. While I care about water purity and the climate crisis, I'm terrified of contamination from native species. *I want it all*, in short, and nature can never win.

3.

Why do women in particular love swimming in rivers and seas? Just now, I run past an advert for a Scottish bank where a woman floats in a freezing loch. I've heard from friends that there are many wild-swimmer women on dating apps. Of course there's the explanation that involves our higher percentage of subcutaneous fat, but surely it can't just be that. There must be more reasons why we swim with all the parasites and pollutants, the oil spills and microplastics. *Is it because we're used to risk?* I wonder, fiddling with the acrylic glue that shimmers gold on my fingers.

Every time I get my nails done, I stare at the masked woman who bends over my hands in a haze of acetone and wish I knew Thai to say *sorry for exposing you, I should know better than this.* Sometimes I remember the mountain of plastic materials I played with and chewed and doubtless swallowed throughout my childhood and I want to dissolve. *Might as well treat myself now*, I think, *before an inevitably messy death.* Then I go months without wearing foundation – not out of pride, but because I'm afraid of everyday chemicals. Phthalates are used to make plastics softer. They're used in nail polish, perfumes, and other forms of makeup. These Endocrine-Disrupting Chemicals, or EDCs, can be found in the outer coating of some medicines and children's toys. EDCs are interlaced with everyone's lives – they're even in 'green' cleaning products – but women are more likely to be exposed, whether they're working as cleaners or doing household chores. Add to this the entanglements of gendered products, like menstrual pads made with carcinogenic styrene. EDCs are linked with increasing rates of breast-cancer in industrialised societies. Another Japanese Breakfast song, 'Heft', is about Michelle Zauner learning of her mother's terminal cancer: the same diagnosis that led to her aunt's death. *What if it's the same dark coming?* she sings. I listen to her worries on repeat and wonder which illness is waiting to meet my mother, my siblings, and me. Then someone compliments my nails and I start the toxic cycle all over again.

4.

Here, in the present, I slow my pace as I hop along the eastern breakwater's uneven stones, weaving between couples and other runners. Later, my Strava map will make it look like I've run on the sea. I pause next to two swearing fishermen to take a picture of the waves and they do not move out the way or smile at me. Maybe it's naïve to romanticise the haenyeo and fishwives. We've reached the stage where the environmental impact of animal agriculture is guiltily acknowledged in the UK, where veggie and vegan options are on most menus; to revere the tradition of fishing seems cringe, at least to younger generations. And yet it feels even worse to forget the enmeshed histories of women and men, water and industry. Sometimes I feel a share of responsibility. The proliferation of plastics, glitters and aerosol sprays from the '90s, from my childhood, led us to where we are today. We want to look young and pretty and yet our makeup may well be what ages and kills us: all the unseen chemicals clogging up our pores and swirling down the drain and out to sea. The same sea where we swim, naturally.

I wonder what the fishwives would make of me, living today just minutes from where they'd slice and fillet fish caught with bare hands – not mass-farmed and cling-wrapped. For some reason I think about stock photographs of women grinning with salad. I imagine the fishermen laughing as I turn back along the breakwater: just another white woman trying to be healthy, to be deep. Here comes the dive. Here I am: piercing my finger on a sea urchin between rocks and sucking out the sting. Here are the chemicals seeping from the pharmacy to clean my body and then pollute something else, entirely. And again: I'm holding my breath when I cycle past the sewage treatment works, as if exhaust fumes are any less dangerous. I think of leathered faces free from make up; long, tight calves. I would like to hold my breath for longer than most men can. Instead I am often out of it, worried about the relation between my body and the land, the waters, underwritten by the glimmer of history. Whoever these women were, I hope they would forgive me. Though it meant something different to them, they knew how to live with impurity. They, too, just wanted to swim free.

References and Further Reading

Bertram, James G. (1866), *The Harvest of the Sea: A Contribution to the Natural and Economic History of the British Food Fishes*, New York: Appleton & Co.

Bracht, Mary Lynn (2018), *White Chrysanthemum*, London: Vintage.

Carnie, Tony (2022), 'Durban beaches pulled out of Blue Flag sparkling sea awards', *Daily Maverick*, 3 November, 18 pars. www.dailymaverick.co.za/article/2022-11-03-durban-beaches-dumped-from-blue-flag-sparkling-sea-awards/ (accessed 8 June 2023).

Criado Perez, Caroline (2019), *Invisible Women: Exposing Data Bias in a World Designed for Men*, London: Chatto & Windus.

Edinburgh Museums (2023), 'Leith and Newhaven', *Museums & Galleries Edinburgh*, 20 pars. www.edinburghmuseums.org.uk/ leith-and-newhaven (accessed 8 June 2023).

Hildyard, Daisy (2017), *The Second Body*, London: Fitzcarraldo Editions.

Japanese Breakfast (2016), *Psychopomp*, Dead Oceans.

Japanese Breakfast (2017), *Soft Sounds from Another Planet*, Dead Oceans.

Newhaven Heritage Centre (2023), *Newhaven: A Stravaig Through Time.* www.newhavenstravaigs.scot (accessed 8 June 2023).

Ratcliffe, Dougie (2023), 'Oysters and the Firth of Forth – Part 1 (Pre-industrial Revolution)', *Maorach Beag: Scottish Shellfish*, 6 February, 25 pars. maorachbeag.scot/blogs/journal/oysters-and-the-firth-of-forth-part-1-pre-industrial-revolution (accessed 8 June 2023).

Ross, Iain (2023), 'Oysters and the Firth of Forth – Part 2 (The Fisher Folk)', *Maorach Beag: Scottish Shellfish*, 23 March, 43 pars. maorachbeag.scot/blogs/journal/oysters-and-the-firth-of-forth-part-2-the-fisher-folk (accessed 8 June 2023).

Ross, Iain (2023), 'Oysters and the Firth of Forth – Part 3 (Extinction & Rebirth)', *Maorach Beag: Scottish Shellfish*, 21 May, 38 pars. maorachbeag.scot/blogs/journal/oysters-and-the-firth-of-forth (accessed 8 June 2023).

Stallard, Esme (2023), 'Sewage spills: Water bills set to rise to pay for £10bn upgrade', *BBC News*, 18 May, 42 pars. www.bbc.co.uk/news/science-environment-65626241

Swan, Asa James (2020), 'Twilight of Newhaven: The Transformation of an Ancient Fishing Village into a Modern Neighbourhood', *Theses and Dissertations – History* 57, University of Kentucky. uknowledge.uky.edu/history_etds/57/ (accessed 8 June 2023).

World Wildlife Fund, 'Restoration Forth', www.wwf.org.uk/scotland/restoration-forth (accessed 8 June 2023).

Tia Thomson
THUS' AIR MO CHUIMHNE

rudeigin mu do dheidhinn-sa
a chur dachaigh na mo chuimhn'

seillean a' srann cùl a-muigh
pìos talmhainn làn grèine, le cat

na laighe mar shnìomh, aon shùil bheag
na dhùisg fhathast, earball is cluas

air an aon ràmh, bodhaig air fad
a' faighinn fois, ach deiseil . . . deiseil.

YOU ON MY MIND

something about you
reminds me of home

a bee buzzing out the back,
pocket of sunny ground, cat

lying a spiral, one small eye
still awake, tail and ear alert

whilst the body rests
ready and waiting . . . prepared.

John Tinneny
923

'Traduttore, traditore'
—Italian proverb

The 923 bus service often translates me
back from Glasgow to Belfast,

down Ayrshire roads, the coastal route, which
is nearly always under repair, or diverted.

Sometimes the bus is near-deserted, sailing
towards Cairnryan, Mary Celeste-esque.

Other days I am elbow to elbow with
American tourists rediscovering their roots,

or a Scottish crowd, like the one led
by Big Gav, dark fruits in hand, belting out about how

he hates Roman Catholics to the melody
of 'I Think We're Alone Now', whose top kept telling me

to remember the Somme, where my great-grandfather fought
for his country, for some reason, building bridges

at Passchendaele, amidst the mines, who woke
screaming in the night for years afterwards.

My favourite part of the boat ride is when
we reach the boat itself. When Scotland slides away,

slowly, the wind farms waving me farewell, and I
feel my nostalgia switch back towards them

like the wind, which beats the bare metal top deck,
where I breathe in sea-air, and feel rinsed, like a washed
        mouth.

I've made the crossing so many times I feel
I've begun to recognise the birds. The albatrosses.

Sometimes I feel I could unfold my arms like them,
feathers revealed like Swiss army knives.

I could become some kind of bird. A swan, probably.
Something like the children of Lir. But willing.

I could drift on the sea for years, waiting
for the next migration. I could disappear here,

if I wanted. And even if I didn't,
I could be disappeared.

A RIDDLE

I am a house that you enter blind
and leave seeing. What am I?

I walk on all fours in the morning, two legs
at noon, three in the evening. What am I?

I say I am 'gay enough' for a pull, and prove it.
You lose me on the dancefloor, and then

find me again on the street, months later,
on the other side of Byres Road,

waiting for lights to change. I'm leaning against
a pole stacked with stickers and labels

overlapping to the point of illegibility.
My name escapes you, unlike the question

that doesn't escape your lips;
'What do you mean by *enough*?'

Answer: Do you really need one?
Wasn't this more than enough?

My hands wrapped around your waist?
And my fingers, resting gently, on your belt?

Jacques Tsiantar
FRUITS OF THE SEA

We should have known the salmon were bad – flinging themselves onto the shore like an exodus from the near freezing ocean, a clamour of silver flank and flashing tails. Father John had the fishmonger lopping off heads and gouging guts. They should have noticed them, then. The worms in their flesh – silken white and wriggling.

*

Elspeth pushed to the front of the crowd, little Rosie swaddled to her chest, her head high to meet the scornful looks she always received. I hung back, a hand around Conrad's collar – he was already too fast for me to catch if he set on snatching a fish. He was never like this before Bran died. When we had hot meals.

Father John talked past Elspeth, to me. Everyone will get some – that was the promise.

'Even you, Gillian,' he said, 'with your harlot sister and her bastard.'

I had to hold Elspeth back, saying we needed to trust him. Harlot or no, his pride wouldn't let anyone in his congregation starve.

*

We slept like we had when we were children, Elspeth and I. Top and tail, in a single bed, our own children in their cots. That night her sleep came with fits – I still have the bruises to prove it. Legs wheeling under the piled sheets before a desperate throwing off of everything, the cold air smacking us both before I set the covers back, pressing a divot around her body. It was no better when she woke, only calming when I promised to secure us some of the prodigious catch.

I found they had turned the church into a smokehouse, its doors open as a trimmed carcass. No greater use for the house of God than feeding the five thousand, said Father John, his face slick

with fish-fat and eyes red and weeping with the smoke. He waxed
lyrical about us all being in salted fish for a year, his dog collar
straining as he delivered his sermon to pews full of curing meat.
Elspeth and I will get our due, he promised.

'That is, if you reconsider my offer.'

He didn't follow me to the candles. I know he thought he needn't.
The church, my house – the entire village was his home. But as I
started to light one, I felt him come up behind me.

'Conrad needs a male presence, Gillian.'

In the miasma of his cloying breath on my cheeks still frozen
from the wind outside, I told him no. A hand shiny with fish oil
reached out and squeezed my arm, kneading my flesh through
my sleeve.

Refusing to recoil, I hardened.

'We are in a church, Johnothan.'

I lit a candle for the four of us and left. John, grinning as if what
he had asked for was coy, receded back to his altar through the
rows of meat.

*

I used the last of our money to buy potatoes and flour, and started
the road back home, each foot crunching through the snow making
it slick and uncertain. My eyes were down, searching for loose
stones, until I heard the sound of something chewing.

A horse blocked the road, loose from whoever owned it, head
down and grazing. As I tread off the road to skirt it, I saw what it
was dining on. One of the salmon, still slapping itself into the
frozen earth as the horse pressed its body into pulp between its
teeth. I found myself stopping in my tracks, and the horse raised
its head to stare me down. Its breath came in clouds, and its eyes
shone with the quiet cunning of a wolf.

I hurried home.

*

More wolves greeted me at our door, wax paper packages of the salmon in hand. Even in the building sleet, the fish oil on their cheeks and lips shone. They gawked open-mouthed as I approached.

'Is it such a spectacle?' I asked. 'A woman returning to her home?'

The fishmonger, the pink of salmon meat under her fingernails – huffed.

'She still with you? The whore?'

'Such a kindness Father John did you,' another chimed in, 'letting you stay in his brother's house.'

'What a home for strays you've turned it into.'

'My husband,' I said, clear and even.

They stopped, then, shuffling their feet like children scolded.

'Bran was as much my husband,' I continued, 'as he was John's brother.'

The snow started blowing sideways, making shrouds over all of us. I gave them and their impotent silence a wide berth, wrenched open the door, and pulled myself inside. A foot stopped it from closing, accompanied by a hand holding one of the wax paper packages.

'Just take the salmon, Gillian,' spat the fishmonger, 'so you can die in the spring, when the ground is softer.'

*

When I was sure they had gone, I opened the package, revealing the meat pink and glistening. Elspeth brought Rosie and Conrad over. I went to unload the last of our food, hearing the wax paper crinkling, before Conrad squealed in his own, infant language.

'Da-mon!'

It was only when I came back, looking over Elspeth's shoulder, that I saw them. What had looked like a line of silver fat started to curl into an ouroboros, before unspooling and burrowing out of sight, within the flesh. Little white parasites, wriggling through the gossamer threads between the salmon's flakes.

I blinked.

Conrad grasped a fillet in his tiny hand, bringing it to his mouth.

I almost shoved Elspeth to the ground to get to him.

'Give it to me.'

He looked up to me, seeing his mother wild-eyed and furious with panic. His little brows knotted, and he broke into a wail.

'Stop, Gillian! There's more than enough,' said Elspeth, but I snatched the meat from her too, and threw the whole package against the wall. It fell with a wet smack, folding down into the dirt.

After an uneasy breath, I told them what I saw, but Conrad's keening wail cut me off. He scrambled for Elspeth, burrowing amongst her skirts. She went to speak, but I shouted over the both of them.

'Did he eat any?'

Her eyes hardened.

'What are we going to eat, Gillian?'

'Did he eat any of that fish, Elspeth?'

'What is wrong with you?'

In the row that followed, I saw that Conrad's screaming mouth was empty. I wanted to grab his face and pry open his jaw – see if I could smell the fish on his breath. But what would I have done if I had?

Leaving all questions unanswered, I locked the door and sat down.

'Help me peel,' I said, taking up my knife and slicing away at the first of our three potatoes.

*

A knock at the door roused us from sleep. I woke to see it was still night, the snow piling high on the windows. An eerie light flickered outside – a false sun that beckoned me to the door, past Rosie in her cot, and Elspeth slumped by the fire, Conrad in her arms.

It was John holding a lantern, the dirty fish-oil flame smoking within it, sheltering under the eaves. His dog collar was undone to allow his bulging neck some room.

'What hour do you think this is?' I asked.

He went to speak, but something gurgled up his gullet. Even in the wind, I could smell the pungent odour of fish on his breath.

'G-Gillian,' he managed. 'I want to apologise – for today.'

He stifled another belch, neck undulating as he swallowed.

'We have decided—'

'Who's we?' I asked.

Between his gritted teeth, I saw the John I knew – not this appeasing façade.

'We have decided,' he continued, failing to hide his fist before it clenched. 'Bastard or not, your niece should be baptised. We are holding a midnight mass – everyone is coming,' he burped again. 'To celebrate the feast.'

'The feast? There's no feast until—'

'There is a new feast.' His voice flared, before settling again. 'You'd be wise to come.'

The smirk came back, like scum forming over stock.

'Unless you want me to make good on what I own.'

He patted the doorframe with an oil-slicked hand, before moving off into the darkness.

*

It was a tense journey down, with Conrad clutched to my chest and Elspeth clinging to my sleeve. The road was lined with them – the salmon, all flopping about. Dogs had broken from their kennels to feast with the cats, their bellies distended and dragging with the meat. One sheep gorged itself on a pile of worm-ridden refuse excreted by a horse, lying belly up and gasping in the snow.

Further in, we saw them flocking to the church – an obelisk billowing with smoke. Everyone, parent and child, their bellies tight to their oil- and bile-soaked clothes, toggles straining, and collars desperately undone despite the freezing wind. Elspeth clutched tighter to my sleeve.

We would get her Rosie baptised and get out.

Anything to keep our home.

It was a congregation of coughs and splutters, the smokeboxes spewing fat clouds of coal-black, viscous fumes. We nestled ourselves close to the door before John heaved himself up to the lectern. He had grown fatter, his belly having burst his shirt buttons and hanging out like an octopus hood, glistening just as much with the drippings of half-digested salmon.

He wiped his mouth before speaking, meat winking between his teeth.

'What is a gift,' he cried, his voice bubbling up amongst the arches, 'if not an obligation?'

A murmur of whispers weaved through the congregation, and John's smile widened.

'What is a bounty, if not a bestowal of life?'

The sound of someone coughing near the front split into a vile retching. Elspeth's hand wound tighter around my arm.

'What's wrong with them?' she whispered.

John drove on through the sound of vomit splattering onto the stonework, not before suppressing a belch of his own.

'What is a home,' he swallowed hard, his neck jostling, 'if not an appointment of stewardship?'

The congregation mewled in agreement, more sounds of belches and groans blooming within it. The smell wafted around us – of rancid fat and waste. John's eyes found us, like two little, imperfect pearls glinting from within clam meat, and he brought his fist down onto the lectern, the crack echoing about the stone hall.

'Our blessings of late are a boon, yes!' he cried, before his voice grew calm and sober. 'But there are those amongst us who forget the price of a gift – and that is gratitude.'

They all started to shift in their seats.

'And what is God if not the bearer of the greatest gift of all?'

I held Conrad closer.

'And what is a refusal of His gifts,' John continued, 'if not a sin?'

Like a hive of rabid owls, their mad-eyed faces all swivelled as one, glaring at us with mad, glossy-faced grins.

'But the ungrateful among us,' John managed, between deep, guttural belches, 'will still be fed.'

We should never have come. I looked back, only to see the doors being heaved shut behind us.

'For God loves us all – even harlots, bastards, and thieves.'

I dragged Elspeth up as the sound of them rising filled the church.

'We're going,' I said. 'Now.'

The doors had been bolted, the iron slick as I tried to draw back the bar.

'Make them eat!' John cried, and the congregation marched towards us.

'Take Conrad,' I told Elspeth, who clutched him to her chest, turning round to face the congregation's wicked, approaching faces. I wrapped my sleeves around my hands, gripped the iron bar, and pulled with all my weight. It slid free, the howling wind rushing into the church as the doors swung open.

Elspeth cried out behind me as one rushed at her. She nestled her foot against his undulating body and kicked, sending him to the floor in a pile. But another weaved around, gripping Conrad's face, a fistful of the salmon flesh in her hand.

A scream burst low and rasping from my throat as I rounded on her, hooking my full fist's worth of fingers into her mouth and throwing her to the ground with a dull crack as her skull struck stone. I snatched Conrad and broke into a run, Elspeth close on our heels.

*

We sprinted as fast as we could to the bay, but the fishing boats had been crushed by the sheer number of salmon that were, again, swarming in their hordes. Sharks, eels, and even squid were amongst them, all clamouring to be eaten.

It was a blessing – the tide of churchgoers behind us being distracted, their roiling bellies pulling them towards the water.

I cast one glance back to see them knee-deep in the tide of fish, clawing raw flesh into their mouths, the hands of those less fortunate reaching out from the melee, drowning under the bounty.

The few stragglers that kept on our tails sluggishly tried to keep pace, before one doubled over, his clothes splitting as the worms now fat, silken white and large as snakes erupted from all orifices. The others slowed to a stop, their ire hooked by the promise of fresh meat, as they crouched down to feast.

*

Door locked behind us, we scrambled for our things. Conrad did not stop wailing, and Rosie joined the chorus too from Elspeth's chest.

'Soon, we'll go soon,' I told him. I had checked him on the way up to the house – his face was smudged with the grease, but I couldn't smell the fish on his breath. Elspeth gathered blankets and lamp oil, stuffing them into a sack and slinging it over her shoulder.

'What else do we need?' she asked.

'Nothing,' I replied, 'Let's—'

It was only then I noticed the wailing had fallen silent. Rosie was bundled quiet up to Elspeth's breast, but Conrad had wandered off to the far corner of the house.

'Conrad?' I called.

He was crouching by something in the dust.

I ran up to him, grabbing him by his tiny shoulders and pulling him back. Clutched in his fist, and smeared around his lips, was the salmon meat from earlier that day, roiling with its worms. He stared at me as he chewed, frantic and ravenous.

It was then that I broke, falling to my knees and blocking my ears from the shrieking cry that I only realised was my own when I ran out of breath, my voice hoarse and croaking in my throat.

'Move,' I heard.

A shadow passed over me as Elspeth's hand moved me gently to the side. I slumped to the floor, watching as she knelt by Conrad.

'I'm sorry,' she said to him, before cradling his face by the cheeks and sliding her fingers into his mouth.

I wept as I saw Conrad start to thrash against her grip, gagging with his whole, tiny body until the glistening meat came up in a rush of sick. I could see them even through the tears – worms, fat and frantic, writhing on the floor.

'We're going,' said Elspeth.

I looked up at her, my body begging me to lay down and let sleep take me – the kind of sleep that had been building for years.

She gripped my shoulder, her hand still wet from Conrad's vomit.

'Now.'

She wrenched me up to standing. I scooped up my still thrashing and wailing son, and we forged out into the cold, only to see a figure wavering in the road – a swinging lantern hooked in a limp hand.

'Gillian!' John cried, 'Give me my nephew, or by God I'll make you bear me a son.'

We watched as he lumbered towards us, his neck bulging so high up his face that he looked like a worm himself. His bloated, oil-slickened fingers fumbled with the lantern, the flame inside dancing madly.

'Go back to your congregation of gluttons!' screamed Elspeth. 'You'd fit right in if you weren't so fat!'

'How dare you, whor—'

He started, before balking, a tide of vomit gushing between his teeth, falling into a steaming, iridescent pile on the ground.

'—Whore!' he finished, breaking into a lopsided, stomping run, bringing the lantern back to swing it at her. Elspeth stood her ground, clutching her hands around Rosie.

'You and your bastard won't see the—'

The lantern slipped, falling from his fingers into the pile of sick he had left. The fish oil gleamed before bursting into a dirty, smoking flame, John catching with it and becoming a pyre of bubbling fat and splitting skin. From within, the silhouette of his body exploded with worms, falling to the burning ground, and blindly winding around each other into a tangled mess of roasting flesh.

I would have stayed there for hours to watch him burn, but Elspeth turned her back on him before taking my arm and dragging me away into the night, her own lantern held high, lighting the way.

*

I can't stop checking Conrad. His crying has quieted to sobs.

'Eat it,' I tell him. 'Please, Conrad.'

After hours stumbling in the dark, we heard the creak of a wagon, the clop of horseshoes on the road. A woman with goods to sell stopped us and asked which way to the village before we told her everything that had happened. Without a word, she ushered us up into the wagon and gave us bread and water, pulling her horse around and starting back the way she came.

Elspeth has fallen asleep, resting on my shoulder in the back of the wagon. I could sleep for a week, too. The hay is comfortable enough, but I won't until I know Conrad is okay. I am all about ready to chew the bread myself and feed him like a bird, but he mercifully starts to eat.

'We'll get you lot to the port,' says the woman. 'There are doctors there who can check you over.'

'Thank you,' I say. 'We can't ever repay—'

She holds up a hand, and I quiet.

'Don't start with all that,' she says. 'You saved me a trip to some-where I don't want to go, by the sound of it.'

We roll along in silence for a minute. Conrad has woken, and grabs the bread in both hands, chewing like a baby hungry for milk.

'The wean doing all right?'

I look up. The woman nods to Conrad, and I smile.

'I think he's all better,' I say. 'Thank you.'

'It's nothing.'

Conrad keeps eating as the wagon wheels creak along, and Elspeth fusses, bringing her jacket round herself and Rosie.

'We don't have much,' I say, breaking the silence, 'But we can give you—'

She tuts at me, rolling her eyes.

'Just think of it like a gift.'

She whips the reins, and her horse presses on as the sleet abates into sparse flakes.

'Last time I checked, they were free.'

Claire Urquhart
DIPPER

The ancient barbecue balances on two good legs,
its rest against the rock-face earned.
Wafts of charcoal and lighter fluid drift
to where the two girls are crouched
digging in the riverbank.

A third, smaller girl is eating,
the vivid green of the crisp packet bright
against her navy top.
The man tends the barbeque, coaxing it
with gentle breaths and tender words.
The woman is unpacking food, certain of his success.

Meltwater hurtles from higher ground,
white taming to murky brown
in the pools below.

The sun is not shining.
On the opposite bank a bunting watches.

Snack eaten,
the littlest one stands up,
only she sees the bunting,
walks towards it,
stops at the water's edge.
The crisp packet crackles as she stoops to fill it.

A splash,
bigger than pebbles thrown.
A shout.
The woman drops

the food she holds
rushes to
the lip of the pool,
jumps in.
Eyes screwed shut,
a handful of navy clothing
clutched to her.

Later in the car,
heater blasting,
neither says
that she landed
on the ledge of a bottomless pool,
that she'd never learned to swim.

EXCHANGE

You give me a hot-water bottle
every evening tucked in at my feet,
light as you
gently open the curtains,
always first to rise.

You never give me carnations,
since her illness, the funeral,
the smell of them rotting and
in return I forgo mushrooms
and (sometimes) blue cheese.

You give me football scores,
election statistics, historical data
in return I share words for
particular colours,
remind you what you chose from the menu
the night we got engaged.

You give me my passport
as we board a flight,
plucked from
your safe-keeping, black, passport-holding pouch and
I let you.

Lynn Valentine
MIDNIGHT, MIDSUMMER, CROFT NA CREICH

Stillness grips the house, just me
and the old dog as I re-read *Longley*
in the living room. No need of lamp
or candle, just silver kettle of sky
as it pours a deluge of light
across firth, field and hamlet.
Swifts still busy on the wing
gathering scattered mists of insects.

Moon and stars are shy as morning,
wide lustre of sky firing the land.
Every tree is molten lava, every puddle
burnished, every blade of grass a spark.
Too soon this place will be drenched in darkness,
winter curtains shut late afternoon, but for now
there is a galleon of pewter and pearls.
The old dog and I sail across the world.

ST KILDA CROSSING

I pulled all my mother's expectations
with me, like a child's kite, giddy with stir
of spring. Because she was cancer-cracked
I turned tourist by proxy, crouched into cleits
looking for leavings of last century.

I photographed fawn smallness of Soays
felt the crash of wind-whipped stacs,
my pockets salt-filled. I leant
on those islands as my mother leant on me,
filled my lungs with their breeze
and leaping green language of sea.

I tried to hold my breath for days,
took it back to my mother, exhaled
island air on her weakened frame –
whispered broken stories of birds and rain.

Lorna J. Waite

WEE MERCURY

Yer wee ball o iron goes backwards tae gie forwards
A gay gords o planetary dance, ma wee freen
Mair celtic metaphors, ye are the forge o ma soul,
The iron blood o star dust, movin wi the flight
O my Scottish mother daein her messages, pullin
The orbit o my sister an myself in a circle
Roon shops, factory, café, nae sittin doon,
Keep movin, nae doodlin, nae messin aboot
Nae keepin time wi mind shadows, nae keepin
Feet still, an endless anxious waggle,
Around our carbon hearth, screams goin up chimneys
Warmin oor nighties afore a sleep
Held up by the cauld dance of violence, a collision o fist
Punchin a crater oan yer face nae man will name

Wee Mercury, wi yer acne marks and potholes,
Craters, pits and speed
I am like ye,
In the hauf shiver cauld o the east
Glaring intae a western settin star
A magnetic field inside points north
Tae the aurora, my wings are silver
Flying beside ravens round the
Radiant sun, fireballs o nuclear reaction
Giein birth to life, yer feet deliver
The message o light, meltin in the atmosphere
Bendin time backwards to recapture lost love.

Wee Mercury, whit message wid ye weep
Wi carbon sympathy when I next orbit the sun
I will place stars upon the soles of my shoes

And run along a ray o light
To surprise you, come up behind.
Earth's anaemic cities carry
Bloodless souls o bloodlines
Making swords from bodies
Dying, extinct ironworks of war
Melt under lavaflows, eruptions of sympathy
For those left behind

Wee Mercury, iron planet
Like tartan, we are all the one stuff.

Catherine Wilson Garry
BESOM

In this life, I put on a black tank top and jeans and boots, and I go to meet Lex at a party at a friend of a friend's flat. I stand in the kitchen and drink lukewarm beer and make small talk with people which I promptly forget. When Lex gets there, we dance to music played out of a set of shitty Bluetooth speakers. I wobble home on my bicycle whilst it's still dark and then the next day I—

*

In this life, I put on a black tank top and jeans, and I go to meet Lex at a party at a friend of a friend's flat. I stand in the kitchen drinking a lukewarm beer and make small talk and the hairs on the back of my neck rise, ever so slightly, and when I turn, I think I see something and the music crackles slightly from those shit Bluetooth speakers. Suddenly, I feel the weight of my mother as she sits on my shoulder saying *better safe than sorry, better safe than sorry*, so I make my excuses and find my bike and wobble home after only being there an hour. I go to bed and then the next day I—

*

In this life, I put on a black tank top, and I go to a party. I take a beer from the communal pile next to the fridge, when a man turns to me.

'I've never heard music sound like this,' he says.

I snort. 'I don't think it's the song's fault, it's the—'

'Speakers?' he offers.

'Right,' I nod. 'Don't think musicians want their music sounding like it's being drowned in a car wash.'

He laughs and opens his mouth to say something, but Lex grabs me to go dance.

'I'm rescuing you,' she whispers. Her breath smells like sweet vodka.

'It was nice to meet you,' I say to the man as she pulls me away, but he's already faded into the crowd. By the time I fall asleep, I have forgotten him.

*

In this life, I put on a black tank top, and I go to a party. Lex isn't there yet, so I head to the kitchen to grab a beer.

'Take this one,' says a man, pulling one out the fridge. 'It's already cold.'

'And they say . . . something about chivalry? I forget,' I say, pulling back the tab.

He laughs. 'Maybe it's dead, but these are reparations,' he deadpans.

'For what?'

'Oh, too many things to count and not enough lifetimes to apologise for them.'

I sip my beer and take him in. I let myself enjoy it. When he says something, I have to lean in to hear him over bass from the Bluetooth speakers someone has set up.

'Listen, I can barely hear you,' he says, shaking his head slightly. 'Can we go outside?'

I nod. Lex never shows up, so there's not really anyone else to talk to anyway. Later, I'd find a text on my phone from her – someone broke into her flat, so she had to wait for the police.

From the garden, the row of houses against the pink sky looks like something from a film. We sit on an old swing set, twirling ourselves round and round so we can talk without anything as direct as eye contact.

'Favourite food?' he asks.

I think. 'Probably pasta. But like, proper pasta. Made from scratch.'

He smiles. 'Did you have some life-changing holiday in Italy or something?'

'How did you know?'

'Just a hunch,' he smiles at a joke only he gets.

'What about you?' I ask.

He looks into the distance. 'A proper roast dinner – the chicken, the potatoes, all the bits with it. My mum makes a cracking roast.'

I take a swig of my beer. 'I'm hopeless at cooking.' I think about the three empty cups of noodles stranded around my flat that haven't yet made their way to the bin.

'Oh, it's easy to learn,' he smiles.

The light fades quickly from the sky and his swing twirls closer to mine until our ropes are knotted together. We fumble trying to detangle them and then suddenly, so suddenly I don't even react, we're kissing. I take the long way home on my bike, enjoying the feel of the night's coolness on my back.

A few days later, we go on a first date. He nervously slops beer down his shirt, and I drop the popcorn on the floor. I wash my hands in a bathroom that stinks of melted ice cream and pink goo soap. The film is supposed to be a rom-com, but the protagonist sets my teeth on edge. When the leading woman tries to break up with him, he wheedles on both knees. I cringe into my seat.

Next to me, he laughs at every single lecherous joke and his laugh is grating and secretly, I wish we just left it at that kiss in the dark garden of that house party, the excitement and dangerousness of it like a sharp knife.

A few days later, his name pops up on my phone. I'm at brunch with a friend.

'Any chance of a second date?' she says.

I roll my eyes. 'Absolutely not,' I turn my phone off and look up at her, but she is gone, her seat empty and—

*

In this life, I meet a man at a party, and we talk about homemade pasta and Italy and his Mum's cooking and then we go on a first date, and it is perfect. I nearly drop the popcorn on the floor, but he catches it mid-air. We watch the first fifteen minutes of a dreary misogynistic rom-com before he looks over at me and we laugh in shared agreement.

'All right, that's enough,' he says and stands up.

'What are you doing?' I ask, looking around to make sure I'm not disturbing anyone behind me.

'I think if I watch any more of this, I might actually die. And I'm guessing that would probably ruin the mood.'

He takes my hand and I follow him.

'Do you fancy lunch?' he asks. I nod and he sets off. We end up at my favourite café.

'How did you know?' I ask, shocked. Later, on the phone to my mum I will say what a wonderful coincidence fell into my life. My mother is older and wiser than I am and does not believe in coincidences, but I can't hear what she's saying.

Soon, so soon, we move in together. I expect to find moving stressful, but he is always one step ahead, always there with a home-cooked meal or cold beer before I get overwhelmed. He comes over to my flat to help. He packages my jewellery so carefully, I almost cry. He takes my grungy tank top out of a donation bag.

'You can't throw this out!' he says, horrified. 'You were wearing it the night we met.'

His love is as fresh and exciting to me as a struck match. I burn when I think of everything he has remembered, everything he has held in his head for me.

When we arrive at our new place, I think *we are nesting*. He puts my old film posters on the wall. I paint the bathroom his favourite colour. We watch old episodes of *Star Trek* and I try to make a shepherd's pie and burn it. We get drunk and sleep on an air mattress. He leaves a recipe book on the counter for me to find.

As a moving gift, his mother gives me a cordless vacuum. I start wearing summer dresses. I go to IKEA and buy new pans. I go to yoga. I learn how to sew. I make curtains. I make soup. For my birthday, he buys me cooking lessons I didn't ask for.

After a couple years, we move to be closer to his family. We swap ambulance sirens screaming through our window for a quiet sleepy commuter town. After he leaves for work, I spend hours filling in forms online instead of just being able to send in a CV. I type out my national insurance number so many times I memorise it.

I walk past a shop window and think the mannequin's dress looks nice and then I realise my reflection is imposed on her empty face. I go to a family reunion and my grandma smiles at what a wonderful young woman I have become.

When I cannot find a job for the fifth week in a row, I start fights. I can feel myself doing it like picking at a loose thread on a jumper. I know this makes me the bitch, because it's my problem and he's not done anything to provoke this in me. I try to stop myself by hiding away in another room, but I can still feel him there. He has already plumped the pillow I fall onto. In the kitchen, he cooks exactly what I want for dinner. Playing from his phone is a new album I listened to today.

When we talk, our conversations begin to stretch in front of me like the dialogue in a video game he has already played where he knows all the answers.

'Why don't you take a break from work?' he suggests, stroking my hair. 'I'm earning enough, you could stay here and take some time off.'

I am so tired of filling in forms and emailing and interviewing over Zoom that I find myself saying 'That sounds nice.'

The next morning, I wake up and realise I have ten hours to fill. Days stretch ahead like a dusty road. I drive around town, drinking iced coffees and reading paperback books in the park. Endless videos of women online, who show me their plastic organisers to organise their plastic possessions. I order paint and paintbrushes, storage containers and cute glasses. When they arrive, I can't even be bothered to unwrap them.

After a few weeks of this, I can tell he's irritated when he comes home and the kitchen is messy, or his parcel is with a neighbour.

'What do you do all day?'

I think back on my day: scrolled on my phone, reheated a tin of soup, had a nap because I couldn't think of anything else to do. I don't have an answer for him.

He flies off to Copenhagen for a conference and I am so bored I get in my car and find myself driving back to the city, no plan of how I'll get back or where I'll sleep if I don't. I call Lex and she tells me about another party at another friend of a friend's and I drink so much that there's no chance of me getting home, not even on the bus. I find my hand in another girl's, clinging to her clumsily. We sneak up the stairs like giggling children and fuck on the pile of coats that has been abandoned in someone's room.

*

In this life, I keep the secret and it eats me alive, like a termite in my lungs.

*

In this life, I tell him what happened and apologise. He is resigned when we go to bed, and it's worse than fighting. I wake up in the night and I can see him, in the garden, walking into the darkness and suddenly he disappears, and I do not know where he has gone.

*

In this life, I go to a party, and I feel this overwhelming sense of déjà vu. But when I try to leave I—

*

In this life, I go to a party, and I feel this overwhelming—

*

In this life, I go to a party, and I meet this kind and funny and generous man. My voice cracks when I tell this story at our wedding. My friends are in matching dresses we picked out in Debenhams and my best friend from school passes around tissues and waterproof mascara. I tell him, in front of everyone, that he is the best thing that ever happened to me, my equal, my best friend and the love of my life. I will spend the rest of my life proving this to him.

We find an old house and rebuild it. I find furniture on the street and refurbish it. I paint the walls. I clean and teach myself to cook with his mother's old cookbooks.

We have two children, a girl and a boy. We get a dog, and the children call him Max after the dog in *How the Grinch Stole Christmas* which we watch every year with hot chocolate on the sofa. I swap a commute for night feeds where my nipples crack and bleed. When I look at the clock, I remember all the times I stumbled home at this time – holding my heels in my hands at 4 a.m., only to get back up for work a couple hours later.

We move to the suburbs so we can have a garden and host barbecues. It just made sense for me to give up my job, because childcare was so hard to find, and he earns so much more. I feel a sense of freedom in not letting anyone down anymore.

One morning, my kids drop their crushed cereal onto the floor, and I sweep out the crumbs with a broom. When I hold its wooden handles in my hands, I think about how it was once a tree – how it probably buzzed with spiders and wasps and flies and rot. Someone stopped that life short and put it to good use.

*

In this life, my husband gets a promotion. We take the girls to Center Parcs for a holiday, and he teaches Alex to swim, and I play with Laura in the baby pool. I hear a child scream and look away, scared it is Alex, but after a minute, I see her with her dad. But when I look back, Laura is gone and I cannot find her, I cannot find her anywhere. I scream his name but he's walking away and will not come and help me.

'It's okay,' he says over his shoulder, 'I'll sort this,' and then he is going to wherever he goes when things go wrong. I try to follow him, but the water is around my feet, and I cannot move.

*

In this life, I am at the park. The baby is still strapped to my front as I keenly push Alex on the swings. Other mums – it is always mums – coo at how big she is, how tall she is getting. Yesterday, she won a spelling bee at school and triumphantly spelled 'carousel' for us for the rest of the day.

'C-A-R-O-U-S-E-L,' she sings as she hits each fence post with a stick as we walk home. I bump the baby in time.

'C-A-R-O-U-S-E-L,' I say too.

We get home. 'How are my girls?' says my husband, tousling the baby and Alex's hair.

'Daddy!' Alex laughs.

'What?' he asks.

'Isaac is a boy!'

I wake up in the night and my husband is gone. I creep to the window and can see him walking towards the bottom of the garden. I rush down the stairs, tiptoeing past the children (?) I can't remember if we have any. I try to sneak up on him, but I trip, and he turns around and—

*

In this life, I open the children's bedroom door to kiss them goodnight. It smells like spilled beer and popcorn and there's a man in the garden and I try to go home but I can't find my bicycle. I dance with Lex but there's a dark spot, a shadow in the corner of my eye and a crackling so loud I shut my eyes. I go upstairs to the pile of coats on the bed, and I fall asleep next to a girl with clumsy hands and I—

*

In this life, we are going to Disneyland. We wake the children in the night with new suitcases and drive to the airport. They are wired with excitement, and it is all too much and one of them cries and I ask my husband to pull over so I can comfort them, but he won't let me. And I know I am lucky. I know I am lucky; I know I am. We are just tired.

But then, they don't eat the toast at the hotel breakfast because it doesn't taste like it does at home. One of them slams the bathroom door and it breaks my toe. I feel pathetic and try to call my mum and she tells me to just come home but the phone line cuts her off. I come into the hotel room and my husband has made the bed and bought flowers for me and I smile, but I know he won't be satisfied because it isn't perfect, it's not what he wants.

*

In this life, I am making sandwiches for packed lunches and the knife falls out my hand. Our dog Max licks the butter off before becoming a cat then shifting back, his claws sinking in and out of his paws, his face shifting between golden and black fur. One eye stays the same shape as a cat's: round with a dark slash of a pupil.

I can't find my husband, but my children run down the stairs crying and their faces flicker before me. They are Isaac and Alex and Laura and a hundred other children I cannot remember the names of. Children who were born and ones that weren't. They look like me, then him, then me, then both of us, then nothing. Where their faces are supposed to be are just holes and I look at them so long I feel myself being drawn in and I walk closer and closer, not even conscious of moving my feet and I—

*

In this life, I am making a packed lunch and I grip the knife and put it in my pocket. The cat licks butter off a slice of bread and I still pack the sandwich for him because there is no way he could know, and I am testing the parameters.

I pretend to sleep but I don't. When I creep up on him, he still hears me but this time, I have the knife and I stop him from going wherever he goes to change us. I stop him the only way I have. I stop him from ever going back to the party.

'I did it for you, you know,' he says.

I wake up and the house is empty. The broom lies on the kitchen floor, broken in half.

*

In this life, I put on a black tank top, and I go to a party, and I drink and dance with my friends and I go home, and the next day is mine.

Ania Zolkiewska

SHRAPNEL FROM KHARKIV

[1]

The air-raid siren went off today while we were in the car. Not
the first time, either. It's why we always drive with the windows
slightly down and never any music. And why there's an ALS
trauma bag in the back. Although, Advanced Life System seems
like a misnomer for a first-aid kit basically designed to stop you
bleeding out.

Based on recent observation the air-raid alarms have a thirty to
thirty-five per cent accuracy rate. So we were informed by Mr G.,
a bearded man with tattooed forearms and a laptop full of photos
of mortar shells, shrapnel and creatively rigged explosives found
in the area.

So, we ignore it. The alarm, that is.

[2]

I have this friend, Behzad, not a friend so much as he's my colleague
and a doctor. He's been doing rounds in the Kharkiv metro for
weeks, every night, for the better part of three months. He
used to be the General Director for a major humanitarian
organisation.

The day we met he was trying to explain to the crewcut cook
why he was unhappy with his oatmeal, '*Bez sakharah, bez sakharah,*
okay?!'

Then to me, 'who the fuck puts Coco Puffs on top of porridge?!
Sorry, sorry. I'm Behzad. I don't get it. Sorry.'

We both stared into his bowl.

[3]

This place used to be a beacon of progress and industry, a city in
mid-capitalist bloom. All flashy cars, cafés and clubs. Flights to
Barcelona, Budapest, Istanbul, Prague, Paris, Sharm El Sheikh, Tel

Aviv, even Kraków. A functioning public transportation system with forty kilometres of metro lines. Now there's barely anybody left and the metro is a giant bomb shelter. Curfew is at seven. And, alcohol is prohibited by order of the Governor.

All the journos left a few weeks ago along with the Russians heading south, chasing the frontline or the cocktails and cappuccinos in Dnipro. Most of the relief agencies are in full remote mode from Kyiv. Or Dnipro. So, they're never here either.

There are people still sleeping in the metro, fewer and fewer lately. A few hundred are holding out in bomb shelters. And some persistent objectors are scattered among the half burnt-out high rises facing east, towards the border.

Like the man on the sixth floor with his sixty-three budgies who receives birdfeed deliveries from local volunteers. His building is charred with smoke. There are mortars falling daily. But he refuses to leave without his birds.

[4]

So Behzad, the doctor with thirteen years of emergency medicine in London, and another five or six playing good Samaritan in war zones, who currently prescribes blood thinners to Ukrainian *babushkas*, turns and says to me, 'I hate doctoring.'

[5]

The sun rises on the still cooling, still steaming fires. The body ache you feel, you now associate with artillery. You haven't learned the difference in sound between 'outgoing' and 'incoming'. Not yet. But you will, soon.

The sirens have just started.

In another week there will be an app that will warn you whenever the air-raid sirens are triggered. Three long wails for incoming. One short wail for the all-clear. You will sleep with your phone. Then you will sleep through the alarms.

You might want to call your mom.

[6]

The metro stations are slowly emptying out. The glass-half-full types ordering construction material. The rest are packing up their Ladas and heading west. Rumour has it that the local authorities want to reopen the metro lines by the end of month.

We're out of artillery range, the mayor says.

[7]

We have taken over what used to be a five-star hotel in the centre of town. All the windows on the ground floor have been filled with sandbags.

Except for our team of medical relief workers and their hangers on the place is empty.

Lunch is served between 12:30 and 13:30. Breakfast is at seven, when the overnight team is back and the day team about to go out. Dinner is at 18:30, unless you are part of the overnight team, then you eat before going out at 16:00, and pack energy bars for the night.

Monthly rent costs about the same as I make in a year.

I am learning not to be upset about that.

[8]

On the news you see that volunteers are pouring in across the border. Women and children are clogging the train stations heading west. Volunteers are heading east. Volunteers for what, exactly? Your president orders men from eighteen to sixty to remain in the country.

You wonder how much money you have left in your bank account.

You wonder if you should have left.

[9]

This is the first warzone where I am addressed as comrade, as prodigal daughter, as co-conspirator. I'm not from here but I speak the language, and my grandparents were born here. Sort of. My mother was born in Ivano-Frankovsk; my father's father, in Tarnopol. Though it was called something else then.

Then the Soviet Union came and they left.

I arrived via Moldova, by road. On the way, the driver turned to me and said, 'Did you ever notice that on the inside of our passports Ukraine is written in capital letters? Not like a normal country – one capital at the beginning of the word, but in ALL CAPS.'

'I did not know that. No.'

'Do you know what that means?!' His head jerked back and forth from the road to my face then back again, his eyes triumphant. 'It means it's a corporation. A limited liability corporation, not a country.'

It is a five-hour drive from Iaşi to Vinnytsia.

[10]

- The Ministry of Environmental Protection and Natural Resources requested the delivery of food to prevent zoo animals from starving during the shelling.
- More than thirty tonnes of food was transported from Austria to Ukraine by train in a single month. Ten tonnes of pellet food and dry hay was brought for elephants, baboons and chimpanzees, giraffes, zebras, and tropical birds; ten tonnes each to Kyiv Zoo, to Kharkiv Zoo, and five other zoos.
- Odessa zoo workers drove eight hundred kilometres across the country to rescue two six-year-old white lions. They drove all night to Kharkiv and returned to Odessa in a day.
- The kangaroos were evacuated from Kharkiv Zoo on 24 March. The orangutans left earlier.

[11]

Roman has been acting as tour guide for the last couple of days, taking me around in his matte-black muscle car. He used to organise parties in a club-café downtown. Drum and bass, mostly. Now he organises food deliveries and first-aid kits to bomb shelters and high rises.

I find myself saying yes to things much easier here than in other places. It's the false friend of a common language.

On our way to Saltiivka, I tell Roman about the metro.

'I'm not a politician,' he says, 'but if you ask me, it's too soon.'

He speaks softly and wears a black baseball cap to match his black cargo pants and black bulletproof vest. He has brought an extra one for me. He breezes through checkpoints. He looks like he knows his way around a tourniquet.

He is the fourth volunteer contact I meet above ground. He goes almost every day to the still-smouldering east side of town. He brings cell phone batteries, power banks, prescription refills, and the more banal food and blankets. Care packages brought to you by the Emissaries of Base.

[12]

There is something grotesque in the damp cellar smell of bomb shelters and the rumble of artillery in the middle distance. If it's close enough but not too close, the kids on the platform will stop to listen and call out. 'Incoming!' 'Outgoing!'

Then they go back to running around with their arms stretched out in front and their hands shaped like pistols. They dive behind benches, dash around pillars, up and down stairs. They close one eye, take aim and mouth 'pow pow'. The adults sip tea and play cards, shuffling in their slippers to the common toilets.

If it's too close, everyone huddles and looks expectantly at the ceiling. In between, they cough. Like during a lull in a symphony concert.

And then there are the mosquitos. The surprising number of mosquitos in the underground.

[13]

I am going through the plastic storage box in search of snacks. We get weekly food deliveries from the west of the country. There is always chocolate, biscuits and instant noodles. Sometimes there is fruit. Someone mistakenly ordered thousands of pizza-flavoured high energy bars. They taste like some post-apocalyptic freeze-dried reimagining of something once known as pizza pressed into a dry pocket-sized rectangle weighing two hundred and fifty grammes.

I am starting to dream of non-wrinkly apples.

Across from us is the Pharmacology Department building of the local university. It now doubles as a warehouse where a group of volunteers collects donations and then picks and packs them into household food and medicine deliveries. A group of drivers does house-to-house deliveries during daylight hours.

Due to shrapnel on the roads, there is a shortage of car tyres.

[14]

You do not see the point of worrying anyone until you know what's going on. Your sense of danger is not quite that advanced. Not yet. Why worry them? It might have been an accident. It could all be over soon.

[15]

When curfew lifts at six, the driver comes to collect us from the metro station. We pack up our sleeping bags, the medical supplies, go to the toilet one last time. I watch Alyona, a twenty-something tiny doctor, open her compact to check her makeup. She has brought wet wipes for her face. She applies just a hint of powder to her nose, chin and forehead; mascara and lip gloss. I admire her sense of decorum.

The stout station master comes out of her office/bedsit wearing her royal-blue vest with reflective strips and waves us off. It is light out and there are people smoking on the stairs at the entrance. It is their doctor-prescribed thirty minutes of sunshine a day.

On the way back in the car I can smell the metro and my own sweat mingling with everyone else's. Alyona shows me pictures of her apartment, her cat.

'Before, I was volunteering in a kitchen peeling potatoes. Imagine! I don't cook. But we needed to do something. So me and a friend peeled potatoes for the Territorial Defense. Piles and piles of potatoes.' She throws her head back and laughs. 'My hands were covered in blisters. Covered. It's harder than you think.'

She scrolls through pictures of her neighbourhood. 'Here.' She pushes play on a video. On screen I see high rises in the pre-dawn light. She takes the phone and holds it to her ear. She raises the volume. 'I took a video, so I would remember the sound.' She looks down at the video. She is grimacing. We are driving, so the only sound we hear is the wind rushing through the windows in the car.

'The first days were terrible. Just constant. Then the windows shattered. The building across from us was hit.' She keeps scrolling. 'There!' She hands me the phone again. 'That's my cat.'

I see a cat with a bandage around its front leg and part of its head.

'Shrapnel injuries. We had to bandage him after the windows shattered. After that we kept him in the hallway.'

She keeps scrolling.

'And these are my turtles. Well, not my turtles. They're in a friend's office close by. I had to go and feed them, make sure they're okay. She was scared they were already dead.'

[16]

Shortly after I arrive in Vinnytsia I am given a health and safety medical briefing. I am asked about allergies, medical conditions,

told who to contact in case I am sick. The guy responsible for the
house shows me the safe room in the event of mortar fire – basement,
or in the event of chemical attack – laundry room.

'Better seals,' he offers by way of explanation.

There are also 'simple and user-friendly' personal decontami-
nation kits in the house in case of nerve, white phosphorus or
chlorine gas attack. Each kit has a foldable gas mask: a clear plastic
hood with a Darth Vader air filter. The doctors have another kit
with drugs.

It's about as reassuring as seeing the drop-down oxygen masks
in an airplane. 'In the event of low cabin pressure, put *your* mask
on first *before* helping others.'

'In the event of a chemical attack,' Holly, who leads the decon-
tamination training, says, 'this hood gives you fifteen minutes of
clean air to get somewhere safe.'

I try to imagine fitting the hood over my head and calmly
checking the seal, while the cloud of toxic gas billows up from
somewhere.

Later, I see Holly count the number of hoods we have left in the
house: eleven.

There are thirteen of us.

[17]

In another few days, you will wonder with a certain childish
curiosity how deep the holes are or how far a shell fragment can
travel? You will wonder if you should cancel your subscription to
the gym? Whether your office is still standing? Or whether you
can still pop down to the store and get more coffee in case you
run out? Then you will wonder how much food you have in
the fridge.

The authorities will first ask then enforce a lights-out policy
from dusk until dawn. So now you have no coffee and no lights.
The batteries in your flashlight don't work.

You don't want to stand next to the windows and the hallway running between the rooms of your flat, the safest spot, is pitch black. Of course, there's still your phone.

You text, and your neighbour brings you cans of soup and candles.

[18]

We are driving across the country again, well kind of. We are driving with petrol we have bought by siphoning from other people's fuel tanks. It's how we manage to build any fuel reserves.

The drives are long and the country is flat. The blue sky is oppressive, overbearing. On the way we stop at gas stations for our 10L top-up and to get hotdogs and tea. The hotdogs are held in a bun designed so ketchup and mustard don't leak out the bottom. Only one end is open. The wiener is cradled in a pocket. Smart, and strangely delicious.

The tea comes from a machine with a QR code. You scan the code and press the button for your beverage. The scanner is never very good. I have to ask for help. There aren't many people driving, so the truckers don't know what to do with the Slavic blonde woman with Doc Martens who can't operate a coffee machine. They are pot-bellied, swollen with hotdogs and too much sitting. But always clean shaven. They remind me of my dad.

I smile. They smile. They take my coupon and try to get the machine to obey. They don't look at me.

Mission accomplished. I say, thank you. They nod and shuffle away.

[19]

The metro in Kyiv has been open for a few weeks. Bono came recently to play on a platform. Boris Johnson was here too. But Elon Musk is the one that everyone remembers. Not because he was here, but because when the Minister of Digital Transformation sent a tweet asking Musk to send StarLink terminals to guarantee connectivity, Musk reacted instantly.

I talk to Michail over WhatsApp at night, or whenever he has signal. He is hanging out with the local administration. He is hanging out with the StarLink boys; it's how he gets internet signal in his besieged town now two kilometres from the frontline. He is staying in a building that used to house a bunch of NGOs before the war, before they all left.

Michail is half Ukrainian, but has a foreign passport. He was visiting friends when war broke out and stayed. The first time I message him, I ask him if he's heard of us.

'Yeah, I know you guys. Everyone knows you guys,' he says. 'I can still see your shiny white four-by-fours in the parking lot, right where you left them.'

He wants to tell me to fuck off, but he doesn't. Instead, the next night he calls again. 'I have a pharmacist here. They can tell you what you need to know.'

He asks me if I could send some asthma inhalers. And mosquito coils.

I look at Behzad. He nods.

I say yes.

[20]

The news trickles in. On your screen, a balding man hunches at a desk and airs his grievances. He is wearing a navy suit, white shirt, red tie. He has decided today is the day.

The legacy of insults and threats (real and/or perceived) has now forced him into a response. Vladimir Vladimirovich Putin has cast himself as the reluctant hero heeding the call to action.

His response is decisive. It descends in arrhythmic booming bass sounds on your stoop.

At this point, you might want to call your mom.

[21]

Michail calls again. 'They are running out of insulin, basic pain meds, adult diapers. Diarrhoea is on the rise.'

'Where are you getting water?'

He laughs. 'There's no water, princess. People are getting water from the river. Unfiltered river water. Look, I have no idea what's going on. I'm not a doctor. You're the doctors, no?'

'The thing is,' Behzad says, 'it's probably the same medical profile as the places around Kharkiv. Old grannies. Blood pressure problems. Prolapsed uterus. Incontinence. Diabetes. Upper respiratory infections. The usual.'

Behzad is our doctor. In case of any emergency, we've all agreed to jump on and protect Behzad. He knows how to use all the medical kit.

'Vitamin D deficiency. If they're in shelters.'

[22]

Behzad is laughing in the backseat of the car, a strong belly laugh. He is laughing at his phone. His girl in London has sent him a funny goat meme. Our driver, Alexey, smiles; I turn around.

'Sorry,' he says. Still laughing, he shows me his phone. 'It's from a friend.'

On the screen are goats hanging, standing, lying against cliffs. Nonchalant at impossible angles. Their heads are turned to look out straight at you. There's a caption but I can't read it.

'It's the deal we have for keeping in touch. She knows if she sends a message like, how are you? you okay? I won't answer. It's not that I don't want to. I just can't.' He grimaces. 'Won't. Put it all into words, say something, soothing. It's exhausting.'

I nod. Hudson looks up, smiles, goes back to his laptop. He does not hear us.

'So she sends me a meme. One a day. Always goats. And when she sees that I've read it, she knows I'm okay. That's it.' He smiles. 'It's been our thing for years.'

Hudson is calculating Aquatabs and water containers for a population of thirty to fifty thousand. I turn back to the front.

'What?' Alexey asks, in Russian.

'It's a friend of his, sending him a joke.' I answer in Russian. I am too tired to play interpreter.

'Friend? Or, lover?' Alexey asks, looking at Behzad in the rear-view mirror.

'Friend. Lover, maybe. I don't know.'

Alexey smiles.

'Checkpoint,' he says in English. He unhooks his phone from the car phone mount. We put our phones away. Hudson folds his laptop and lays it on the floor.

[23]
- The Ministry of Defence tweets on official channels, 'Ukrainian soldiers love cats.'
- Celebrity cat Stephan, a tabby with more than a million followers on Instagram, is appointed as Ukraine's cultural heritage ambassador.
- Patron, the bomb-sniffing dog, is given a service medal from the President and immortalised in a stamp.
- Academics debate the significance of this latest social media wartime phenomenon: Dr Ian Garner points out the emotional humanising effect. We know who the good guys are. They seem nice, they have these adorable animals on their side.

[24]
You wake up in the dark early morning to a soft rumble, almost thunder, but it's February and lightning storms are rare this time of year. Soon you realise that the sound is deeper, much more destructive – the sharp impact of something hitting the ground. Its aftershocks are absorbed and reverberate in the soil, against the foundation of your high rise.

The night is otherwise quiet, but you are now awake. From your window on the tenth floor you see the tracers in the pre-dawn light. Now what?

If you reach for your phone to call your mom,
go to section [14].

If you turn on your phone to see what you can find on Telegram,
go to section [20].

Or maybe you try to go back to sleep. Maybe you're dreaming.
You'll figure it out in the morning. Go to section [5].

BIOGRAPHIES

Shasta Hanif Ali is a writer, poet and anti-racism campaigner. Her writing delicately navigates the legacy of migration, race and heritage; where themes of memory and language interlace and disrupt. Her work has been published in *Sidhe Press*, *Books From Scotland* and the anthology *Our Time Is A Garden* (IASH), among others.

Henry Bell is a writer, editor and poet based in Glasgow. He is the author of *Red Threads: A History of the People's Flag*, alongside three chapbooks of poetry. He runs people's history tours of Glasgow with Radical Glasgow Tours and is a committee member of the Red Sunday School.

C. D. Boyland is a [d]eaf poet, visual poet and editor. His debut collection, *Mephistopheles* (2023, Blue Diode Press), has been described as 'a work of desire, refusal and ardent storytelling'. His pamphlets are *User Stories* (2020), and *Vessel* (2022). He is currently co-editor of the *Glasgow Review of Books*.

Colin Bramwell is from the Black Isle. He was the runner-up for the 2020 Edwin Morgan Prize and won the 2018 John Dryden Translation Competition. His poems and translations have been published in *PN Review*, *Poetry Review*, *Magma*, *The London Magazine* and elsewhere.

Eve Brandon lives in Glasgow. They work in archives and keep busy writing horrid little stories. Their most recent work has been featured in *CloisterFox* and *The Crow's Quill*. You can find them on X (formerly Twitter) at **@EveBrandon_**

Nathan Breakenridge is a Scottish writer. His stories and poetry have previously appeared in *Pushing Out The Boat*, *Neon*, *Gutter*,

Not Deer, *The Horla*, *New Writing Scotland* and *Shooter*, as well as the anthology of strange tales, *Mooncalves*. He was shortlisted for the Scottish Book Trust New Writers Award in 2019.

Nathaniel Cairney is an American poet of Scottish descent who lives in Belgium. His chapbook *Singing Dangerously of Sinking* was a finalist for the 2021 Saguaro Prize in Poetry, and his poems have been published in *The Cardiff Review*, *Moria*, *Broad River Review* and other literary journals.

E. E. Chandler is a writer from Aberdeen whose work has appeared in print in several publications, including *Poetry Scotland* and *Pushing Out The Boat*. Having recently taken early retirement to commit more time to writing, she is working on a memoir about her former career although she prefers writing poetry.

Rachel Clive is a writer, theatre practitioner and researcher based in Glasgow. Rachel has had poetry published in *Poetry Wales* and in various pamphlets, print anthologies and websites. Rachel's main literary output is plays, often written collaboratively or through experimental theatre practice as research processes.

Claire Deans is originally from Glasgow but currently lives in Dumfries. She has had her poetry and short stories published in various literary magazines including *Skinkling Star*, *Cutting Teeth*, *Gutter*, *Poetry Scotland*, and *New Writing Scotland*. She is busy redrafting her first novel along with a collection of short stories.

Lara Delmage is a writer whose work delights in folklore, intersectional feminism, queerness and animals working with poetry, theatre and film. Her poetry has been published by *Osmosis Press*, *Little Living Room* and *Heroica*. She is currently working on her debut short film, *Sissy Puss*, and a full-length play, *Banshee Baby*.

Tha **Johana Egermayer** air a bhith ag obair mar neach-rannsachaidh agus eadar-theangaiche. Dh'ionnsaich i Gàidhlig nuair a bha i san oilthigh. Tha i a' fuireach ann an Alba. Nochd cuid de na dàin aice ann an *AIMSIR* (Samhain 2023, **aimsirpress.org**).

Graham Fulton has had twenty-seven full-length collections produced by many publishers including Polygon, Penniless Press, Red Squirrel Press, Seahorse Publications, Pindrop Press, Smokestack Books and Salmon Poetry. The latest is *System: Special Edition Selected Poems 1986–2023* (Published in Silence Press, 2024). He used to play drums and run marathons.

Niamh Gordon (she/her) is a writer and researcher undertaking a PhD in Creative Writing and Narrative Studies at the University of Glasgow. Her fiction, poetry and essays have featured in publications including *Flash Fiction Magazine, Return Trip, Strix* and *The Polyphony*. She's also a Research Assistant for the DeathWrites Network.

Zoë Green has won a Candlestick Press prize, been shortlisted for *The London Magazine* Poetry Prize 2022, was highly commended in the Scots category of the 2023 McLellan Poetry Prize, and was longlisted for the 2023 Winchester Poetry Prize. Her poems have been published by *Atrium*, Candlestick Press, Coin-Operated Press, *Ink Sweat & Tears, The Interpreter's House, The London Magazine, One Hand Clapping, Poetry Salzburg Review, Pushing Out The Boat*, and Sidhe Press.

Lydia Harris has made her home in the Orkney island of Westray. Her first full collection, *Objects for Private Devotion* (Pindrop), was longlisted for the Highland Book Prize. Her second collection, *Henrietta's Library of the Whole Wide World* (Blue Diode), has just had its launch in Westray and also in the Orkney Library and Archive.

Benjamin K. Herrington (bkh) / wears many masks and speaks in many voices / looks for hidden messages _ v e r _ w h e r _ / feels incredibly grateful to have had his poetry and prose published by *The Prairie Review* / *La Piccioletta Barca* / *B O D Y Literature* / *Granfalloon* / *Apocalypse Confidential* / sculpts stories / paginates poems / runs Lake Michigan shorelines / is working on a novel and seeking gn0s1s.

First-time author **Michael Hopcroft** has been researching the local history of Renfrewshire for over fifteen years. Living in the village of Lochwinnoch, he has a particular interest in the role of landscape in both shaping human history and in offering us a means of connecting with our past.

Ellis Jamieson is a queer, non-binary, neurodivergent writer. Their work has been published in *Shoreline of Infinity, Briefly Write, Bacopa Literary Review, Parliament Literary Journal, Coin-operated Press*, and on Yorick Radio. They're the winner of the Prose Purple Flash Fiction Award (2023) and were longlisted for the Emerging Writer Award 2023.

Ioulia (=Julia) **Kolovou** is a Greek-born, Glasgow-based author. She studied Classics and History in Greece, Linguistics in Argentina, and Creative Writing in Scotland. Her biography of the medieval princess and historian Anna Komnene was published in the inauspicious spring of 2020; her debut novel, *The Stone Maidens*, in 2022.

Ruby Lawrence is a writer and performer based in Glasgow. Her poetry has been published by *Propel, Gutter, Pilot Press, The Moth* and others. In 2023 she was shortlisted for the Out-Spoken Prize for Performance Poetry. You can find her here: **@ruby_lawrence_o**

Hannah Ledlie is an Edinburgh-born, Manchester-based writer interested in form and futurism. In 2015 she was shortlisted for the

BBC Young Writers' Award and in 2019 she was a winner of Penguin's 'Platform Pride' spoken word competition. Her work has featured in *Ambit*, *Porridge*, *Gutter*, and *Magma*.

Kate McAllan is a visual artist and writer based in Glasgow. Her work has appeared in numerous literary publications including thi wurd's anthology of fiction and experimental writing *Alternating Current* and Belgian literary journal *Deus Ex Machina*. She is currently developing an illustrated collection of short stories.

'S ann à Dùn Dèagh a tha **Donnchadh MacCàba**. Tha a chuid sgrìobhaidh air nochdadh ann an *Causeway/Cabhsair*, *New Isles Press* agus *Poetry Scotland*. Mar as trice, bidh e a' sgrìobhadh mun àrainneachd, eachdraidh is cruth na tìre ann an ear-thuath na h-Alba a bharrachd air tachartasan na bheatha phearsanta.

Hayli McClain is a Pennsylvania-born writer now living in Stirling, Scotland. She was shortlisted in the 2022 Brilliant & Forever festival in Stornoway, and her stories have appeared in places such as *NonBinary Review*, *Reflex Press*, and *Luna Station Quarterly*. She's for hire as a freelance editor and does natural monoprinting in her spare time.

Jennifer McCormack grew up in Glasgow, where she studied Arts and Social Sciences at the University of Glasgow and Art and Design at Langside College. She lives in Malmö, Sweden where she was first published by *Ordkonst* magazine in 2023.

Rowan MacDonald lives in Tasmania with his dog, Rosie, who sits beside him for each word he writes. Those words have been published around the world, including most recently with Sans. PRESS, *Red Ogre Review* and *Dipity Literary Magazine*. His short fiction was awarded the Kenan Ince Memorial Prize (2023).

The ninth poetry collection from **Crìsdean MacIlleBhàin / Christopher Whyte**, *Athair / Father*, in Gaelic with facing English translations by the author, will appear in autumn 2024. An eighth book of translations from the Russian of Marina Tsvetaeva, *Roland's Horn*, with poems from 1917 to 1925, will appear from Shearsman Books early in 2025. An anthology in Gaelic and Italian, *Non dimenticare gli angeli*, won the Premio Rilke in September 2023 and a selected poems with Catalan translations by Jaume Subirana and Francesc Parcerisas is in preparation. He currently divides his time between Budapest and Ferrara.

Carol McKay's poem 'Ceilidh' was named one of the twenty Best Scottish Poems in English in 2022 by the Scottish Poetry Library. Hedgehog Press published her pamphlets *Reading the Landscape* in 2022 and *None of This Makes Any Sense* (in collaboration with Keith McKay) in 2024. Her website is **www.carolmckay.co.uk**

Gordon Mackie has worked for the Fife library service for fifteen years. During this time he has encountered a broad spectrum of human existence from which he draws inspiration. His reading to writing ratio is approximately 10,000:1 so don't expect to hear too much from him.

Jane McKie is a prize-winning poet who has written several poetry collections, the most recent of which is *Carnation Lily Lily Rose* (Blue Diode, 2023). She currently convenes the Edinburgh-based Shore Poets, a monthly evening of poetry and song.

Iain MacRath / Iain Macrae was brought up in Harris but is now based in Glasgow where he works as an actor and writer. His drama writing has been produced on stage, BBC television and radio. His poetry has appeared in numerous publications, including *Poets' Republic*, *Poetry Scotland*, *Scotsman* and *New Writing Scotland*.

Luke Mackle is a writer from the Clyde Valley who works as a political economist specialised in industry and climate-related reforms in the countries of the former USSR. He currently lives in Paris with his wife, Jessica, and their two dogs, Gibson and Marcel.

Emily Munro is a writer, filmmaker, and curator based in Glasgow. Her work has been published internationally in a range of journals, zines and anthologies. She was longlisted for the 2023 Caledonia Novel Award.

Raised in Ness, Isle of Lewis and now living in Shetland, **Donald S. Murray** is a Gaelic-speaking poet, author and occasional dramatist. His novel *As the Women Lay Dreaming* won the Paul Torday Memorial Prize for 2020. His latest novel is *The Salt and the Flame* (Saraband).

Sindhu Rajasekaran (she/her/ள**) is an author, filmmaker, and academic. Her novel *Kaleidoscopic Reflections* was longlisted for the Crossword Book Award, while her latest book of non-fiction is the critically acclaimed *Smashing the Patriarchy*. She is currently working on her PhD in Creative Writing at the University of Strathclyde.

Martin Raymond's stories have appeared in *New Writing Scotland* and *Causeway/Cabhsair*. They have been shortlisted for a number of awards, including the V. S. Pritchett Short Story Prize. His novel *Lotte* will be published in September 2024. He has an MLitt and PhD in Creative Writing, both from the University of Stirling.

Aimee Elizabeth Skelton is a Scottish woman who loves to write. She has an MA in Creative Writing and Education from Goldsmiths and has contributed poetry and research to various literary journals and anthologies. She currently lives in Glasgow where she works for a charity and facilitates writing workshops with adults learning English, children and young people.

George Smith's first novel *Chrysotile Mice* was a response to his father's death. It remains unpublished. Currently, he is writing a collection of short stories. George has published in *The Drouth*, has written chapters in books from Edinburgh and Oxford University presses and is co-editor of *1820: Scottish Rebellion* (2022).

Morag Smith's poetry has won or been shortlisted for numerous prizes and published in magazines and anthologies, including *Poetry Ireland Review*, *The Scotsman* and *Gutter*. Her pamphlet, *Background Noises*, about the rewilding and human history of the semi-derelict Dykebar Psychiatric Hospital near Paisley, Scotland, is available at **redsquirrelpress.com**

Caitlin Stobie is the author of *Thin Slices* (Verve Poetry Press, 2022) and *Abortion Ecologies in Southern African Fiction* (Bloomsbury Academic, 2023). Her latest publication is a collaborative short story collection with Kharys Ateh Laue, forthcoming in 2024. She teaches creative writing at the University of Leeds.

Tia Thomson was raised in Glasgow with strong Highland roots, is long settled in Nairn, and is a member of ForWords writing group. Currently working with Gaelic Early Years and teaching piano; loves the rhythms and patterns in poetry, playing with words and ideas. Creative activities are even more important these post-Covid, pre-Independence days – but it's coming yet :)

Born and raised in Belfast, **John Tinneny** has had work appear in *From Glasgow To Saturn*, *Channel*, and *Comhar*, and was also longlisted for the National Poetry Competition 2020.

Jacques Tsiantar is an award-winning, disabled, Edinburgh-based writer. His work tackles illness, gender, grief, and the uncanny.

He won the 2024 Dinesh Allirajah Short Fiction Prize and was shortlisted for The 2022 Bridge Award's Emerging Writer Award and the 2016 MMU Novella Award. He is currently writing his debut novel.

Claire Urquhart grew up in Carnoustie, Scotland. A product of the 80s Scottish education system, decent exam results and a fear of blood meant she ended up studying law in Edinburgh where she now lives. Twenty-five years later she found her way back to poetry and began writing herself.

Lynn Valentine lives in the Scottish Highlands. Her debut poetry collection, *Life's Stink and Honey*, was published by Cinnamon Press in 2022 after winning their literature award. She is working on her next collection for Cinnamon Press.

Lorna J. Waite (1964–2023) was an educator and an activist. Her collection *The Steel Garden* (2011) and her PhD research explored the destruction of heavy industry in Scotland and its social consequences. 'Wee Mercury' was written while she was writer in residence at Hugh MacDiarmid's cottage at Brownsbank.

Catherine Wilson Garry is a poet and writer. Her debut poetry pamphlet *Another Word for Home is Blackbird* was published in 2023 by Stewed Rhubarb Press. Her work has been featured by BBC Radio 4, the British National Gallery, *Extra Teeth*, *Gutter* and elsewhere. She is a member of The London Library's Emerging Writers and the Push the Boat Out Festival team.

Ania Zolkiewska left Poland as a child, shortly before the Berlin Wall fell. For years she worked as a humanitarian in various countries in Africa, Central Asia, Europe and the Middle East. She lives and writes in Edinburgh.